"One day we'll do much more than kiss," the marquis said

And Sophia, mortified at her warm response to his kisses stolen in the antechamber of the ballroom, failed to note the teasing tone in his voice.

"Sir!" she exclaimed. "You simply must stop tormenting me like this."

"But it's quite a good sign that I torment you, you know," stated Carrisbrooke blandly. Then with a connoisseur's eye he made a small adjustment to Sophia's dress, disarranged by the embrace, and tucked a curl back into her headress. "Gives one every reason to expect our liason will be a pleasant one."

With a tortured "Oh!" Sophia turned on her heel and fled back to the comparative safety of the ballroom.

MISS DALRYMPLE'S VIRTUE

MARGARET WESTHAVEN

Harlequin Books

TORONTO • NEW YORK • LONDON
AMSTERDAM • PARIS • SYDNEY • HAMBURG
STOCKHOLM • ATHENS • TOKYO • MILAN

To Anne

Published April 1988
ISBN 0-373-31021-8

CHAPTER ONE

SOPHIA DALRYMPLE TORE the crested letter into four neat pieces and scattered them on the sun-dappled floor of the dining parlour. "I swear, Papa, I'd give my virtue if it would get my novels published," she exclaimed in vexation. "I'm certain we've tried everything else."

"Now, now, Sophia, drink your coffee," advised the Reverend Mr. Dalrymple, as with his usual mildness he applied himself to his tankard of mead. "You don't mean it." He smiled in most unpriestly appreciation of his daughter's wit.

"I most certainly do," retorted Sophia. "What else, pray, might we try to get me into print?"

The vicar frowned in thought; but his grey eyes were twinkling behind the spectacles, which were often lost, and more often than not discovered perched atop the reverend gentleman's head. "We might solicit another patron," he suggested.

As Mr. Dalrymple had expected, this comment brought a disgusted and most unladylike snort from his daughter. "We've asked for help from the most remote of our relations who have any pretensions to influence in Town, and they've been uniformly odious," she said with a pout. "And this letter from Lord Bell, our last hope?" She indicated with a wave of a slender hand the shreds of paper on the polished oak floor. "He hadn't even the decency to respond in person, merely had his secretary write you that his lordship hasn't the time or inclination to concern himself with the matter. His secretary, indeed! Oh!" Her smoky grey eyes flashed.

"The baron was a very distant connection of your mama's, and she's been gone for five years," the vicar reminded his child. "It isn't surprising that such a busy man, whom we've never met, would choose not to use his influence on behalf of what might be, for all he can guess, the amateurish scribblings of an untalented schoolgirl. He doesn't know you, Sophia, and he hasn't an inkling of your ability."

"But I read your letter to him, Papa," protested Sophia. "You told him I was gifted. You said such wonderful, complimentary things." Remembering, she smiled fondly at her sire.

"And what father wouldn't say such things of his child?" countered Mr. Dalrymple. "Simply because they are true in your case, my dear, doesn't mean that my correspondent could know that. No, I think we should look out a patron who is familiar with your work."

"But there is no such person," cried Sophia, nearly shouting in frustration at her papa's obtuseness. "You know very well that only you and Miss Helver have ever seen my work."

"True. And that is why I'm proposing you show it to someone else."

"Whom?"

"Why, the lord of the manor, of course," stated Mr. Dalrymple. "Carrisbrooke."

Sophia's eyes widened, and an observer might have noted how very large and thickly lashed they were, really the most attractive features of the lady's pretty, perfect oval of a face. Her pale skin and cloud of dark hair were relegated, thanks to those eyes, to the position of secondary beauties. Unfortunately, Sophia's sole companion this morning was her father, the Reverend Mr. Dalrymple, who was above such worldly things as physical appearance.

On this particular sunny summer morning the two were breakfasting in the comfortable, somewhat shabby dining room of the old stone vicarage. The dining parlour was a pleasant chamber, its well-worn furniture polished to a high shine with beeswax and lemon. Sophia, a young woman of four and twenty in a very old round gown of white muslin, was sitting opposite her father, rotund and jocular-appearing, and dressed in an extremely shabby—but well-brushed—coat of rusty black. A man of some sixty years, his most outstanding feature was his fine head of white hair, and if there was any resemblance between the father and daughter, it was in their nearly identical keen grey eyes—though in Mr. Dalrymple's case their effect was not so much of beauty as of intelligence.

The thoughts of both Dalrymples turned to the marquis of Carrisbrooke. This nobleman was the absentee landlord of Oakley, the large estate whose park skirted the vicarage garden, and whose village was shepherded by the Reverend Mr. Dalrymple and his curate, Mr. Penn. The marquis had come into the neighbourhood but once, long ago, upon inheriting Oakley Park. At that time the vicar and his lady had met him, though Sophia, still of schoolroom age, had had no more than a brief sight of the new owner.

"You know that Carrisbrooke went to Paris last month with his regiment, after Waterloo," said Sophia. "And besides, he never comes to Hertfordshire, even to see his sister. Why, I haven't so much as glimpsed the man since I was sixteen, and we've never met."

"All that is true, my dear," returned her father, "which is why I propose that you act through his sister."

Lady Amarantha Burroughs, who lived at Oakley Park, was a woman of means and fashion whom Sophia, as the spinster daughter of an impecunious clergyman, had never felt able to befriend, though the two often discussed parish matters. Sophia had always suspected she would like Lady Amarantha if she got to know her, but as things stood, the mere thought of soliciting the lady's help was daunting. Lady Amarantha owed nothing to Miss Dalrymple, and the thought of putting herself under such an obligation didn't please Sophia at all. Why, she had never even really liked the thought of owing a favour to any of her relations! No, it was impossible.

However, in the interest of family harmony, Sophia promised her father that she would consider his idea. Then she got up from the breakfast table, leaving the vicar to scribble out a sermon over a last rack of toast, and went about the business of her day. The care of Oakley parish busied Sophia quite as much as it did the vicar; perhaps even more, for Mr. Dalrymple had employed a curate five years before and had shifted much of his parish work onto that young man.

His daughter, who had taken on her mother's tasks on the good lady's death, had no such advantage. But she was well able to manage her time. Today she had no parish visits to make; she and the maid had finished the great wash the day before; and the major obstacle which lay between her and the peace of her writing desk was the care of some Seville orange wine that had begun fermenting only last Christmas. Wine making was a special talent of Sophia's, and she always handled both it and the mead personally. She was in the cellar drawing off the orange wine from a wooden cask into bottles when the maid of all work peeked down the stairs to announce visitors.

"It's Miss Burroughs and Miss Helver, ma'am, and I said you was bottling the wine and would they please to sit in the front parlour while I fetch some of my fresh queen-cakes."

"Quite right, Dolly, I'll be there in a moment," was Sophia's cheerful answer. She had soon corked the last bottle and was clattering upstairs in her pattens, removing a patched apron as she went.

Although Dolly had put the callers into the best room in the house, it echoed the atmosphere of genteel poverty that reigned in the dining room: the chintz was faded and the woodwork scarred, but everything was sparkling clean and polished to a high shine. Echo Burroughs, a small blonde miss of sixteen whose close bonnet and simple dress proclaimed her to be still in the schoolroom, was already making inroads into Dolly's plate of queen-cakes. Miss Delilah Helver, the young lady's governess and a plain, matter-of-fact maiden of five and forty, had taken the opportunity to admonish her charge and counsel moderation. "Your mama is always telling you that ladies of fashion have delicate appetites, my dear," she was saying as Sophia entered the room.

"Next year, when I am a lady of fashion, so will I," stated Echo, taking another cake, "if it is necessary. Oh, good morning, Miss Dalrymple. What a lovely lot of currants Dolly's put into these. They're delicious."

Sophia greeted both ladies warmly and urged the sylphlike Miss Burroughs to devour all the cakes she wanted. "Never having been a lady of fashion, I can't be sure if their appetites are always small," she said with a twinkle at Miss Helver, "but I've heard that nearly any eccentricity may be brought into fashion. Echo's habit of gorging and remaining slender as a reed might be more envied than deplored. Especially if she becomes the toast of the Town next year, as we know she will."

Echo dimpled and slipped another cake into her pocket. "I know you ladies want to prose on about books and things," she said with a sigh of barely concealed boredom, "so mayn't I go into the garden, Helvie? Perhaps I can find the cat."

The young lady was instantly given permission for this exercise, for the two older women did prefer to have their discussions in private. Echo bobbed a little curtsey and slipped through the French doors into the old-fashioned vegetable and flower beds that surrounded the vicarage.

"She's going to make straight for the new peas, my dear," said Miss Helver, "and you'll be lucky if she doesn't strip every vine. But I suppose you know that already."

Sophia laughed. "She's such an artless little thing that I can't be cross with her. And Dolly is too much in awe of rank to run her off, though we were planning to have peas for dinner. I'm so glad to see you this morning, Helvie. Papa has had another of his inspirations about my new manuscript, and I need your advice on how to talk him out of it. And," she added, remembering with a smile her own frustrated remark about her virtue not being too high a price to pay for publication, "you must tell me if his idea is as good as the one I've had myself."

Miss Helver, assenting readily, smiled in a fond way at her former pupil. The two had become acquainted when Sophia had attended a ladies' seminary in St. Albans, where Miss Helver used to teach. The friendship had begun slowly, but one day Miss Helver had found herself the recipient of a shy request to critique the young girl's first long manuscript, a distinction which had pleased the teacher very much when she learned that Sophia's only audience up to that time— and she had been scribbling since the age of ten—had been her parents. Miss Helver had picked through the more lurid of the young girl's imaginative writings to find a rare talent in some deceptively simple sketches of village life among the clergy and gentry. She had encouraged the young writer in this direction, and Sophia's attempts at fiction had been improving ever since.

Miss Helver's friendly interest had been repaid, for when Lady Amarantha Burroughs came into Hertfordshire and expressed a need for a governess for her young daughter, Miss Dalrymple had not hesitated to recommend her old friend. In fact, it was entirely due to dear Sophia that Miss Delilah Helver had been delivered from the genteel hell of a teaching position in a young ladies' seminary into the soft and comparatively free life of preceptress to an unexceptional young ninnyhammer who had been relying on her looks since birth—and getting away with it.

Miss Helver admittedly didn't find much of a challenge in forming the intellect of young Echo, who, if she thought of books at all, considered them in terms of their colour and weight; but the chit was sweet tempered if feather headed, and the salary Lady Amarantha paid was generous in the extreme. And it was a true happiness to be so near her dear Sophia, and thus able to share with the young lady's father the honour of being the only people to have read her three completed novels.

"Two ideas in one morning," Miss Helver said now. "I wonder if either can be better than the one I've long had myself."

"And what one is that, Helvie?"

"Why, that you should marry, Sophia, so that your husband can act for you. For you know that he will be rich and influential."

Sophia laughed. Helvie was always putting forward the facetious idea that a rich gentleman was going to drop from the sky and carry her young friend off to a life of wedded bliss. "Yes, rich enough simply to have my novels printed," she agreed cheerfully. "As I'd do myself if I could lay hands on a penny. It isn't something that can be attempted on a dress allowance of twenty pounds a year. Then," she continued with a faraway look in her eyes, "I suppose he'd puff it to all his acquaintance—the haut ton, of course—and I would awake, like Lord Byron, to find myself famous. Except that you know I wish to be anonymous. 'By a lady' has such a nice sound, and I do think it is more genteel. Do you think my fictitious husband would be against anonymity and use his well-known name to publish my works by subscription? And of course he will be well-known."

Miss Helver shrugged and said, "I'm certain he'd be respectful of your wishes, dear."

"Well, that's a comfort," retorted Sophia. "I hate it when imaginary gentlemen fail to live up to my expectations. The fact is that I'm single and likely to remain so, and I'm no closer to my goal. Oh, Helvie! I'm getting desperate."

Sophia's father, if he could have heard her speak so strongly, might have lectured his daughter on the vainglory of worldly accomplishments. He was proud of her, and anxious for her sake to see her words appear in the traditional three slim volumes. But he was not privy to one important cause of her anxiety for publication.

"Dear Father," Sophia said with a sigh. "If only he weren't such a sweet unworldly lamb. I'm certain it's never even occurred to him that when he dies I'll be left to my own devices. He can't save money, you know, and if I don't do something to secure my own future I'll end up on the charge of the parish."

Miss Helver, rather alarmed at the gloomy turn the conversation was taking, hastened to reply. "It's unfortunate that your dear father isn't as forward thinking as he might be, but his mind is on higher things. And besides, Sophia, you are such a lovely girl. The vicar can't be blamed for thinking a gentleman is bound to marry you someday."

"I've arrived at the decrepit age of twenty-four without that happening," said Sophia in a bitter voice. "No, Helvie, my only answer is to get my writing published. What else could I do? Make a living with my needle? I *can* sew, but hardly fast or well enough to keep from starving. And as for being a governess or a teacher in a school, I'd rather die! I've been mistress of the vicarage for five years now. How could I get used to taking orders from others?''

"There's no need to rip up at *me*, my love," Miss Helver broke into these grim musings. "I know you're not suited to teaching. Besides, how would you write if you had to do any of those things? Sewing would take all your daylight hours, and your eyesight, sooner or later. And as a governess or teacher, you'd be at your employer's constant beck and call.''

"Exactly!" cried Sophia, her eyes shining with...was it fear, or anger at her own poverty? "How would I write? I...I must write, you know, Helvie.''

"I know." The governess patted her friend's knee. "And that's why a rich husband is the very thing you need. With his influence to bring out your novels, and his wealth to give you leisure—"

"Helvie," Sophia broke in, a warning note clear in her voice. "A rich husband is the very thing all of us need. But do be sensible." Sophia was as romantic as the next young woman, but she had long ago faced reality. Marry? When the only prospects that had ever come the way of a penniless vicar's daughter were too dismal to be borne? That horrid widower from St. Albans, with his even more horrid brood of screaming children in desperate need of a firm hand; the revolting young squire Sophia had met on a visit to a friend, a man who had seriously suggested that it would be great fun to run off to Scotland with such a pretty girl, but they must count on being cast off by his family for such a misalliance; not to mention the most recent and most annoyingly persistent suitor of all...

"Marriage is out of the question." Sophia sighed, preferring not to dwell on the last gentleman on such a fine morning.

"The right young man won't let a lack of fortune stand in his way," insisted Miss Helver.

"The right old man, you mean," Sophia said, laughing. "We both know I'm at my last stakes. No, I shall somehow manage to write, and years from now, if I should outlive Papa, you and I will rent our little cottage and be as happy as larks. Now, do you want to hear what my enterprising father thinks I should do to secure a patron?"

"What? Ask another relation?"

"We really have none left. No, Papa thinks I should ask Lady Amarantha Burroughs to read my book, and then, if she likes it, I might ask her to tell... her brother about it."

Miss Helver clasped her hands in delight. "Mr. Dalrymple is so clever! The marquis of Carrisbrooke must have no end of influence in the proper circles, and more than enough money to risk a few pounds on your little venture."

"But I hate to ask a stranger, through only an acquaintance, for such an important favour," Sophia explained. "I'm hardly an intimate of Lady Amarantha's, and why should she bother with my concerns? I wouldn't expect it of her, and so I think Papa's idea is out of the question."

"Oh, but won't you think it over?" Miss Helver entreated. "Lady Amarantha is kind and generous; she'd help you."

"I make no promises," Sophia said after a little silence. "Now, don't you want to hear *my* latest thoughts on the matter?" Her eyes sparkled as she remembered her joking idea of earlier. "Since I've tried everything else, I suggested this morning to Papa that

I might trade my virtue to get my novel printed. What do you think of that?''

A peal of laughter from the staid middle-aged lady was her answer, for Miss Helver, though the very heart and soul of respectability, was as used to Sophia's bold statements as was Mr. Dalrymple. ''I admit it's out of the ordinary,'' she said with a chuckle. ''You would go to London, I suppose, and present yourself in the offices of a suitably lecherous publisher?''

''Something of that sort. How do you suppose one finds out which publishers *are* lecherous?''

What Miss Helver might have had to say on this subject was never revealed, for at that moment Dolly, the maid, burst into the room. She was breathing hard, and her cap was askew.

''Oh, Miss Dalrymple,'' she cried, ''I've just heard the news in the village. The marquis has arrived in Oakley! Jem at the Crown saw him ride by on his horse. Only think, ma'am, I might see a real marquis!''

Miss Helver hadn't heard of such a visit; the marquis must have decided to surprise his sister. The governess asked Dolly for details, which the maid was quite eager to give.

As for Sophia, she remained silent, but there appeared on her face a calculating expression rarely worn by a vicar's daughter. Perhaps she would also soon see the marquis. Would he be as handsome now as when she'd had that brief glimpse of him so many years ago?

CHAPTER TWO

"I FAIL TO SEE why you think it is so absurd," said
Lady Amarantha. "Good Lord, brother, you're two
and thirty. You've had ample time to sow your wild
oats, which heaven knows you've done thoroughly,
and your nearest heir is a second cousin. Of course
you must marry." Her fine dark eyes glared disap-
provingly at the lounging figure on the sofa opposite
her chair.

A hearty laugh was the only answer vouchsafed her
for the moment, and Lady Amarantha Burroughs devoted herself to a careful scrutiny of her wayward
younger brother, Charles, who was known to his
troops as major and to the rest of the world besides her
irreverent self as the most noble marquis of Carrisbrooke. He was a handsome man, acknowledged the
lady ungrudgingly; it might even be said that he was a
masculine version of herself, and *she* was still an accredited beauty.

Both Amarantha and her brother had waving hair
of a dark chestnut colour—his in a carefully tousled
crop—and brown eyes of a peculiar intensity and intelligence, set off by finely arched brows. The face of
Charles was naturally more roughly hewn than that of
the classically lovely Amarantha, but still the resemblance was strong and not diminished by the contrast
of his bronzed skin with her glowing white complex-

ion. She was a tall woman, with a stately form; he was a towering figure of a man, powerfully built. Yes, the marquis of Carrisbrooke was a very good-looking male, thought his sister with pardonable pride, and his determined avoidance of parson's mousetrap had devastated many young women and their mamas, almost as much on account of his personal attractions as of his title and estates.

"I've been in England a mere forty-eight hours, Amarantha, and I won't have you vexing me for at least another seventy-two," said Carrisbrooke now with another laugh. "Not after the warm expression of brotherly devotion which this visit denotes. Do you scheme to marry off all your house guests? I'll give you some hope of seeing me riveted, though. When you take my little niece to Town next year to bring her out, I give you leave to try your matchmaking arts on me as well as her for the entire season."

"Cold comfort," Amarantha said with a snort. "That's nearly a year away, and you know I'll be busy with Echo the entire time I'm in London. I anticipate nothing but trouble with that child."

"Why so?" queried the marquis. "She seems a biddable-enough chit to me."

Lady Amarantha sighed. "Oh, she's well-behaved enough now, I'll warrant you, but she's still in the schoolroom and has never seen a young man. Though Echo seems to be all mildness, my mother's intuition tells me that a very lively young thing is about to burst forth once she finds out she's a beautiful woman. She has no idea, you see. And you must have noticed how pretty she is—the image of poor Mama, all blonde curls and dimples—and even though that style of beauty isn't much in vogue, a certain breed of callow young man is bound to go wild over her.''

"Which could only be good, I take it, since you'll be bringing her to Town to marry her off.''

"It is not my desire to pitchfork my young daughter into matrimony in her first season," responded Amarantha with dignity. "I want her to enjoy herself next year, to look about her and gain assurance. But don't you see, brother, that the sort of young tulip certain to be attracted to Echo's looks and to, er, her artless personality, isn't what I'd be likely to call an eligible *parti*? I'll be lucky if she doesn't run off to Gretna Green with a penniless third son or a half-pay officer of the rank of ensign.''

Carrisbrooke laughed again. "I won't have you impugning the honour of half-pay officers, as I'm one myself," he said. "And you're borrowing trouble a year in advance, which isn't like you, Amarantha. Echo will surprise you and have an army of titled, respectable gentlemen of a certain age lining up at the door to carry her off.''

"Well, the problem of Echo aside," Amarantha said, essaying a return to her former theme, "it isn't as essential that a sixteen-year-old girl be married as it is for her rapidly aging uncle. Now do be sensible!''

"I'll be sensible when I'm forty-five. Have done. I've promised to let you have a go at leg-shackling me to one of next season's debutantes, and that's all any fond sister can expect," said Carrisbrooke. His eyes were still twinkling, but a certain tone in his voice recalled the military side of his nature and made his sister give over—for the moment.

"Very well, I'll wait, but I will carry my point, Charles," said Amarantha in pretended resignation.

"So you aren't hanging out for a wife. What on earth *do* you plan to do, now the war's over? You've concentrated on nothing else for years. You'll be bored after a month in England, now that you don't have your battle plans to spread out all over the house and your fellow officers to huddle together with over the latest plan to stop Boney in his tracks."

This was a theme the marquis had indeed given much thought to, and one on which he was quite ready to expound. "Why, what should a respectable landowner do but improve his lands?" he said in a matter-of-fact tone, pretending not to notice the stare of disbelief that had appeared on his sister's face. "For the past six months or so I've kept a valise full of pamphlets on scientific farming at my lonely bedside..."

He paused momentarily as his sister snickered at the idea of his hours of repose being lonely. Tales of his amorous exploits were bound to have reached Amarantha, and she was no prude.

"And," he continued rather severely, when her moment of hilarity had passed, "I warrant you'll find me as great an authority as any other gentleman farmer on crop rotation and crossbreeding. Which practices, along with several others, I mean to see put into effect here at Oakley, as well as my other estates. Satisfied?"

Amarantha was staring in wonder, for she could hear the seriousness in his voice. "You, Charles, a gentleman farmer? Good gracious, then I needn't worry about pressing you to do your duty by the line. Setting up a nursery will be a natural succession to this bucolic turn you propose to take. Are you really to become a model landlord? You've hardly looked at

your land before! I find it hard to credit, but Digweed
will be elated to take you over the estate and show you
the books. As you know, I've taken on many deci-
sions myself, having to do with cows and tenants' roofs
and such things, and you won't find Oakley in too bad
an order."

"I shall certainly see Digweed—a model steward,
I'm sure, and a land agent of rare talent," said the
marquis. "And I've no doubt you've held up your end
as well, my dear sister. You always did have a businesslike streak. I can still remember you as the first
cent-per-center I ever ran across, loaning me your pin
money when I was all to pieces."

Lady Amarantha chuckled at the memory. "And
how many boys of nine could find themselves at *point
non plus*? I think we were both precocious, in our innocent, endearing ways."

The two reminisced a bit more about their child-
hood, touched on projects currently in train at Oakley and exchanged what they knew of ton gossip—
which was quite a lot, Lady Amarantha just having
come from Town and his lordship from Brussels by
way of Paris. They had not seen each other for
months, ever since Carrisbrooke had gone off to the
Low Countries the previous March in the wake of
Bonaparte's escape from Elba.

They were sitting in the morning room of the Park
on this fine day, the very day of Carrisbrooke's arrival. No one, not even Dolly at the vicarage, was
more surprised than Amarantha at this visit from her
brother, but she was very pleased to see him. Finally
their conversation showed signs of winding down, and
Carrisbrooke noted the longing looks Amarantha was
casting at the lending-library novel on a nearby table.

He excused himself to tour the gardens, and in the next moment, after he had passed through the French doors into the rose walk, Amarantha had dived for the first volume of *Treachery, or The Grave of Antoinette*.

The marquis's highly polished Hessians crunched over the gravel paths, and he was soon making a vigorous circuit of the kitchen gardens, stables and other outbuildings that surrounded the Elizabethan manor of Oakley Park. He knew that until Amarantha's arrival six years before, when her husband Sir Hugh Burroughs had died and she had found herself displaced by Hugh's heir, the place had been virtually uninhabited for years, for Great-Uncle Powell, an archaeologist, had spent most of his time digging about in foreign parts. Amarantha had been delighted to accept her brother's offer to live in one of his minor country homes.

Carrisbrooke had never paid much attention to Oakley, save for a dutiful look round eight years previously, at the time of Uncle's death, and the only thing about the place which had piqued his interest was an amusing encounter with a pretty village wench he had discovered up a tree in the orchard. He still chuckled at the memory of that country lass and her mortification at being turned off the property by the marquis of Carrisbrooke himself. The young creature had probably never before encountered a soul in the deserted orchards of the neglected manor.

Well, Carrisbrooke had to admit as his walk returned him to the old-fashioned walled flower garden at one side of the house, Oakley Park wasn't a place of neglect today. The combined energies of Amarantha and the excellent Digweed had given it back its air of plain but prosperous respectability. The changes he himself planned for the home farm would add to the estate's value and make it a fitting gift for Amarantha. The marquis's design was to make the place over legally to his sister, for her husband had left her no land. And he knew she liked having a place in the country, even though she was in the main a denizen of London.

Carrisbrooke, lost in thoughts of clover and corn, rounded the corner of a magnificent yellow climbing rose tied to a white-painted trellis and nearly ran into a demure female figure in a grey pelisse and a dreadful straw bonnet. The young person sketched a hurried curtsey and almost fled down the path toward the garden door, leaving the marquis to wonder at her identity and muse on the extraordinarily fine grey eyes that had peeked out from the concealing poke of that outmoded piece of headgear. A maidservant, perhaps? The girl was hardly dressed well enough to be anything else. She couldn't be Echo's governess, for Amarantha had already given her brother a glowing report of that efficient, middle-aged individual. Shrugging, the marquis walked around yet another corner in his progress toward the house and came upon a prim woman of a decidedly governessy aspect seated on a bench.

"Ah, you'll be my niece Echo's preceptress," he said in greeting, making a bow so gallant and charming that the prosaic Miss Helver blushed. "I'm Carrisbrooke. You're hiding from the chit, I take it? Can't say I blame you." He grinned in his most engaging way.

Miss Helver demurely stated that her little pupil was all that could be wished, and that of course she wasn't

hiding from the dear child. She had merely taken the
opportunity to entertain a visitor of her own while
Echo was in the kitchen.

"Begging food of the cook, you mean. Still stuff-
ing herself like a Christmas goose, and no plumpness
to show for her trouble?" The marquis chuckled.
"No, please sit back down, ma'am." For the governess had risen nervously to her feet to curtsey. "So
you've had a visitor? Perhaps it was the very shy
young woman in grey who just thundered past me.
Seemed to be on her way out. A friend of yours?"

Miss Helver nodded. "Yes, the vicar's daughter,
Miss Dalrymple," she said. "She just walked back
with Miss Burroughs and me from the vicarage, but
she couldn't stay long." Noting the unmistakable hint
of interest in his lordship's voice, a wild, nay audacious, thought entered her mind as she continued,
"She and I are great friends. In fact, it was she who
got me this post with your niece, my lord. Such a
charming young woman—Miss Dalrymple, that is.
And Miss Burroughs, too, of course." The governess
dropped her eyes to hide their sudden matchmaking
gleam.

"Charming, yes," the marquis answered in a negligent, offhand voice that quite dashed Miss Helver's
momentary hopes and made her chide herself for a
romantic fool. It had always been her plan that a suitable gentleman would be so taken with Sophia's love-
liness and intelligence that he would cast prudence
aside and offer marriage. However, it was a sad fact
that the marquis was so far above Miss Dalrymple's
reach as to make any hopes in this direction the utmost fantasy.

Bidding good-day to Miss Helver, Carrisbrooke continued into the house the way he had gone out, through the French doors into the morning room. His sister, absorbed in her reading, acknowledged his presence with only a nod, and he settled back down in his former position and picked up a book from a nearby table. He was soon fidgeting in the manner of a bored schoolboy and inwardly cursing the dullness of country life.

After a while Lady Amarantha noticed his restlessness and looked up from her novel. "Charles, if you're looking for a way to keep busy, you might consult with Digweed this morning. Or you could make your duty visit to the vicar. I'm sure Mr. Dalrymple would be extremely glad to tell you how matters stand in the parish. He's a very charitable soul, by the way, and it makes one feel positively selfish to see how he works night and day. Do take care to avoid his curate, though. That young man is an encroaching mushroom."

Carrisbrooke shut the volume of Robert Burns he had been perusing and snapped to attention. "Ah, yes, the vicar. Right you are, Amarantha. A visit would be only good manners on my part. Can't expect the man to come to me; he probably hasn't the time, toiling in the vineyards of the Lord and all. I'll hasten over there."

And without further ado the marquis tossed aside the book of poetry, rose and straightened his perfectly fitted morning coat of Bath cloth, and made for the door again with his most determined stride.

His sister looked after him in amazement. She had never thought Charles would take her half-teasing suggestion seriously.

CHAPTER THREE

CARRISBROOKE REMEMBERED from his previous visit to Hertfordshire that Oakley Park was bordered on one side by the vicarage garden, and that a small gate led through the hedge on the property line, no doubt built as a convenience to social intercourse for two families of a previous generation. In his capacity as the then new lord of the small manor, he had noticed the gate because he had felt it might give an ill-advised right of way to idlers, though further investigation had revealed the vicarage property to be so well bounded by hedge and fence that only the vicar's family would be likely to use the gate, and they were certainly beyond reproach.

The marquis headed now for the remembered opening, across a lawn that was being scythed by a young gardener's boy, through the ornamental oak copse that gave the Park its name, and up to the small wooden gate in the high privet hedge. As he had expected, it was unlocked.

On the vicarage side the marquis hesitated and looked about him. There was a tangle of trees at the bottom of this garden: a gnarled apple, an oak or two, a twisted holly. A little farther along the way, a brick path led up a small incline to a sundial, where it was to be supposed the official garden began. Beyond the sundial the worn stone walls of the vicarage could be seen.

Casting his eye once more around the old shelter-ing trees, Carrisbrooke considered the wisdom of abandoning his mission while this shrubbery still hid him from the view of those within the house. Had he been foolish to think of paying a visit to the vicar? And on his first day in Hertfordshire?

And then his eyes riveted to one spot. There was a hammock tied between two of the ancient hollies. Even more interesting, this improvised chaise was tenanted by someone.

Carrisbrooke moved to within full view of the hammock's occupant and smiled. From the grey pe-lisse, and the dreadful bonnet laid on the grass to one side, the sleeper would be the vicar's daughter, the charming and seemingly shy young woman who had so aroused his curiosity—he admitted this freely—that he had forthwith made his way to the vicarage and chanced a possibly lengthy session with an altruistic man of God in order to glimpse her again. The eyes beneath the bonnet had been his major reason for doing this; they were closed now, but the rest of this Miss Dalrymple was tantalizingly on view.

She must have only just fallen asleep. A book clasped loosely in one hand, she was arranged in the hammock in an attitude that could only be described as wanton. The Quakerish pelisse had concealed a simple white muslin gown that did not look new, but was nevertheless cut in the prevailing low-necked, high-waisted style and had the shortest of sleeves. The diaphanous material clung to the wearer's fine figure in several interesting places, outlining her legs and re-vealing the slim curve of her waist. Her dusky hair was unbound and surrounded the delicate oval of her face like a dark cloud. Her hairpins, the marquis noted with amusement, were still clutched in her fist.

A spirit of deviltry overtook Carrisbrooke at this point, and without pausing for rational thought he leaned over the hammock and planted a lingering kiss on the young woman's white brow. He followed this with another one, even more lingering, on her mouth.

Sophia started awake, gave a little gasp and tumbled out of the hammock. "Sir! What does this mean?" she said shakily as she accepted perforce her attacker's hand to assist her to her feet. "Are you mad— Oh!" Her wide eyes suddenly met the amused brown ones of Carrisbrooke. "You're the marquis," she proclaimed in an accusatory tone. "I saw you in the garden at Oakley Park this morning." She didn't add that she had accompanied Miss Helver and Echo back to the Park earlier that day because she had hoped such an accident would occur; nor that she had been too shy to take advantage of that moment in the garden of the manor.

Carrisbrooke bowed. "Miss Dalrymple, I believe?" he said in his best tones, which in combination with his handsome features had never yet failed to inspire flutters in the most recalcitrant of female bosoms. He smiled down at the young lady, a glow of admiration lighting his face as his eyes ran approvingly and rather too boldly over Sophia's figure. "You must forgive me, I was overcome by your charms. *La belle au bois dormant,* as it were."

Sophia merely nodded in a dazed way. She didn't immediately give him the outraged set-down he had fully expected to receive, and indeed knew he deserved. Mauling a vicar's daughter was not in the usual

style of even such a rakish character as Carrisbrooke
serenely knew himself to be; and nothing but her un-
consciously provocative pose would have led him to do
it.

Miss Dalrymple continued to stare at him, and
Carrisbrooke coughed. "Didn't mean to startle you,
you know," he added contritely. Good Lord, was the
chit half-witted? As he considered this annoying possibility he couldn't help a continued appraisal of her
person. She was a tall young woman, her head reaching just past his shoulder. Wavy black hair curled
around her face, and in back reached down to her
waist. Her pale, delicately tinted face, with its straight
little nose, well-moulded mouth and those amazing
eyes, was truly lovely. The girl was a regular dasher, in
fact, a diamond of the first water, and properly
dressed would rival any accredited beauty the marquis had ever met.

Little did Carrisbrooke know that the young woman
standing transfixed before him had been carried back
in time to an occasion eight years in the past. Sophia
had not always been every inch the proper lady. As an
adolescent she had indulged in many a mischievous
scheme, to the despair of her mother. One of her favourite excursions was to the neglected orchard of
Oakley Park, where she stole plums. On one memo-
rable day she had been discovered in the act by none
other than this very man, who, she had later learned,
was making his first tour of the estate. A pit had
dropped down on his head, in fact, and he had forthwith chased the little thief off the property. Sophia had
been too frightened to say a word at the time, and
she'd let the gentleman continue in his mistaken idea
that she was a cottager's daughter, rather than con-

fess that the vicar's only child made the poaching of
fruit her favourite sport. She had never forgotten the
marquis, for he had been quite the handsomest young
man she'd ever seen in her life. She realized now that
he hadn't lost the entitlement to that superlative in the
intervening years. In fact, seeing him in person was
causing her heart to lurch as oddly as it had all those
years ago.

It suddenly occurred to Sophia that, of all the suggestions made that morning about her future, only
one—hers—had made perfect sense. She thought
quickly. The idea would either shock this gentleman
or please him, but she really had nothing to lose.
Heaven knew she had everything to gain. And it was
quite possible that she would never have to follow it
through completely. . . .

"You did startle me," she began slowly, "but I'm
glad you're here. I need to talk to you, Lord Carrisbrooke." There! She couldn't retreat now.

"Do you indeed?" inquired the marquis. His keen
eyes searched the lady's face, and she blushed. "Is it
a parish matter? I was just going to see your father,"
he added, not really believing that a discussion of
church work was at issue here.

"Well, no," said Sophia. In desperation she looked
at the mossy ground, trying to pluck up her courage.
"It's a personal matter. You see, sir, I write novels."

"Novels." The marquis was growing more confused by the minute. First this presumably proper
young female had failed to chastise him for most im-
properly assaulting her in her father's garden; now she
was telling him out of the blue that she wrote novels.
His brows drew together in a frown. He had obviously stumbled into the company of an eccentric,

though beautiful, bluestocking, and he had never had much taste for such women, with the exception of his sister. "Novels," he repeated in mystification.

Sophia nodded. The thought passed through her mind that he was only the third person that she had informed of her secret pursuit. For although a scattered few of her relations—those who had refused to help her—knew about her work, she had never met any of those people, and their knowledge of her affairs couldn't affect her personally. "Yes, novels," she said. Leading the way to a rustic seat under an oak tree, she dropped upon it and motioned to the marquis to place himself beside her. He did so.

Amazed at her own daring and its success—fancy one's own self ordering about a marquis!—Sophia continued, "I write novels, and I believe that they're worthy of publication. My father and I have asked everyone we know of to assist me in this goal, and everyone has refused. Papa and I are quite without money or connections, you know, and our distant relations—Lord Bell, for one—perhaps naturally haven't wanted to bestir themselves in this matter. But it is very important to me to get my work published and bring in a little income, for you know my father can't live forever, and I'll be quite thrown on my own devices when he passes away. I'm trying, you see, to save myself from the governessing trade." She paused and smiled in a way that she hoped was flirtatious.

The words had come out in a rush, and Sophia thought with a twinge of guilt that such a personage as the marquis of Carrisbrooke, who had just come here from the wars and no doubt planned to involve himself in affairs of state and the upkeep of his substantial holdings, would likely have no interest at all in her little problems. She was momentarily ashamed of annoying the great man with such trivia, but in the next second she was reminding herself sternly that her financial problems were not trivial to her, and that this was in fact a matter of life and death. And if she could find a way to earn some money from the sale of her novels, she wouldn't need to ask anyone for a favour ever again. And this wouldn't even be a favour; it would be a...a form of barter.

It would cost the marquis almost nothing to fling her manuscripts in the direction of a publisher in London. As for his being repaid in kind, well, she would worry about that later.

"I see," Carrisbrooke was replying with that same keen, searching look which had disconcerted Sophia for the whole length of their interview, "you wish my patronage. Is that it, ma'am?" He turned his eyes away, kind enough to hide from the young lady his anger at her presumption, and more than half resolved not to reward it by acting for her. In his position, people were always asking him to do this or that; and it annoyed him mightily that this lovely, if odd, young woman was only another such supplicant.

"Yes, I do," Sophia stated bravely. "But I'm aware that I have no claim on you, and it wouldn't be right to ask you to take on my problem for nothing. I...I'm not asking for charity, my lord."

The marquis surveyed his companion with a new interest. "Then you're of a mind to pay me?"

"Yes," said Sophia in a choked voice.

To her horror, Lord Carrisbrooke gave a chuckle that seemed to be full of a ribald awareness of her notion of payment. "May I ask what you have to offer?" he inquired.

Sophia had cast down her eyes again. Had she been looking directly at the marquis she might have noticed that, though his voice was deliberately rakish, his own eyes were full of open friendliness and a teasing concern. However, she did not see this, since she was concentrating her attention on the worn toes of her kid slippers.

Voices from earlier in the day were filling Sophia's mind and echoing in her scarlet ears. *I'd give my virtue,* came her own words, speaking playfully to her father. *The marquis is here!* came Dolly's shriek.

"I have only one thing to offer," Sophia finally said, speaking loudly over her phantoms. She was surprised at how easy this was, for by this simple sentence, which the gentleman must understand, she appeared to be casting away her honour, and, at least initially, it hadn't hurt at all. Perhaps the troublesome rapid beating of her heart, which she knew was caused by Lord Carrisbrooke's nearness, had something to do with this.

Would he accept her terms? Sophia could see no reason he wouldn't. She knew enough about the world to have learned that aristocratic gentlemen were always having intrigues. If the marquis found her attractive—and she knew she was pretty—what would stop him from acting as he had no doubt acted dozens of times before, if the stories about him had even the germ of truth?

Carrisbrooke took Sophia's hand in both of his. "I collect that your virtue, as it were, is the price you have in mind, my dear." He was trying very hard to keep back a nearly overpowering urge to laugh in her endearingly serious face. "The wicked marquis and the gently reared young innocent. Is that the plot of your novel?'' he couldn't help asking.

Sophia blushed to the roots of her hair. "You think my wits have gone begging," she sighed, pulling away her hand, "and I can't blame you. Perhaps they have. But you must know, my lord, that only the knowledge that I'll never marry has led me to be so . . . so incredibly bold. I'm four and twenty, you know, and penniless. If I give you my . . . my . . ."

"Honour. Purity," suggested Carrisbrooke in a carefully serious voice.

"Yes. Well, I'm not likely to miss it. My life is planned, you see, and marriage isn't a part of that plan. There is no prospective husband in the wings, who would be irate on finding I was not a . . . a . . ."

"Virgin," prompted Carrisbrooke, enjoying her shocked look at his utterance of the word.

"Though I would engage you to keep the matter secret, between you and me, as I hope to live out my life in this neighbourhood, and naturally I couldn't stay here if it were known I'd been ruined," Sophia continued in desperate embarrassment.

"*And* by the wicked marquis," put in Carrisbrooke with a chuckle.

"Lord Carrisbrooke, I never called you wicked," protested Sophia. But she could, of course, see the humour in this situation, and she accordingly let a laugh escape her.

The two sat side by side in silence for a moment, the minds of each working with an almost audible activity. "Well, what do you say?" Sophia finally asked. Her own courage delighted her; he might have been gentleman enough to let the subject drop without further mention, but she would not let that happen—

could not, when she was this close to her heart's desire.

Carrisbrooke's thoughts had been running in several directions, all of them amusing, and he knew precisely what to say to this brash and blushing young lady. "Very well, ma'am, I accept your offer. At the advanced age of twenty-four, I don't wonder that you consider yourself unmarriageable, and it would be a true shame for such beauty and life as you possess to dwindle into spinsterhood without knowing... without, er, you understand what I mean."

Sophia did, though she would have died rather than admit that such a consideration had indeed flashed through her mind when she had conceived of this rash act. The prospect of living her whole life without coming within arm's length of the tender passion had caused her much regret since it had become clear to her that she would never have the opportunity to marry unless it were to a man whose touch disgusted her; and she had been plagued by more than one of those. But the marquis! He had filled her secret dreams for eight long years!

"I'm no novel reader, though. You must allow my sister to read your manuscripts and judge their merit before I take action," the marquis went on. "If Amarantha says your work is worthy, I'll take it to London and get it into print. And after it appears, you and I will enter into a discreet and pleasant—nearer connection. I'll engage at the time, in writing if you so desire, to provide for any consequences of our proposed folly."

Sophia gasped. Even if she were forced to go through with her desperate offer, she had given no thought to the possibility of bearing a bastard child.

Carrisbrooke prudently ignored her gasp and continued, "Naturally, our bargain will remain between you and me. I would never be so dishonourable as to publish your shame, and you needn't fear that it will ever be known that you are anything but a sedate spinster lady. Amarantha and the world need only know that I'm giving you my patronage, as the daughter of a vicar whose living is in my gift. Now, do I have your hand on it?" He extended his own, an aristocratic though sun-bronzed paw that seemed inordinately large and strong to the suddenly frightened eyes of Sophia.

But there was no backing out of the arrangement now. As firmly as she could, she shook his hand.

Carrisbrooke then stood up and bowed in front of her. His eyes still held a glint of amusement, which was, Sophia judged, only to be expected. How many times had he entered into a liaison with a country spinster? "We had better get it straight, my dear, precisely what your payment is to be," he said seriously. "Did you have in mind one single scene of passion? I must own I'd prefer a more leisurely sort of affair with you—a country interlude, perhaps. However, we can think of ways and means as the time draws near."

Sophia looked down at the ground, too overcome with embarrassment to make any answer.

The marquis reached down and patted her shoulder. "What, timid all of a sudden?" he said in a rallying tone. "I believe that books must go through a fairly slow birthing process; you'll have plenty of time to get used to this idea. Which is, you must admit it, ma'am, your own."

Sophia met his friendly gaze and essayed a little smile. "You're right, my lord. Shall I go now to retrieve my manuscript? I believe I'll give you my latest one for your sister to read. I think it's the best.'' She stood up—

—and instantly she found herself grasped in the rough embrace of the marquis. He was kissing her with a ruthless force, and she responded as best she knew how—which, as it was the first kiss the very correct Miss Dalrymple had ever received aside from Carrisbrooke's more chaste salute as she lay in the hammock, wasn't any too expertly.

Carrisbrooke held her a little away from him and smiled, an odd light in his dark eyes that the nervous Sophia supposed was either passion or lust, and quite possibly both. "I was going to ask you what made you bargain so easily with something not many gently reared young women would choose to part with," he murmured, "but there's no need for me to do that after all. Such a fiery nature as yours, my love, must often be inconvenient in a clergyman's saintly daughter." He brought his lips down on hers again. After a very long time it was she who pulled away, deeply disturbed, her skin flushed becomingly.

"I'll go to fetch my manuscript." Sophia stepped out of his arms and began to walk as sedately as she could manage toward the house.

"One moment, my dear," called Carrisbrooke after her retreating figure.

She turned back, her face still flaming. "Yes?"

The marquis grinned and moved nearer to where she stood. "I would have been glad to lend you my help in your project without exacting your honour as payment, you know," he said in a confidential manner. Then he actually winked! "Now, of course, it's too late. We've shaken on it."

Sophia gave him a stricken look and ran up the path. She was out of earshot by the time Carrisbrooke found himself unable to contain his glee any longer. He burst into whoops of unrestrained laughter.

CHAPTER FOUR

THE VILLAGE OF OAKLEY was one of the most pleasantly situated hamlets in Hertfordshire. Nestled in a small valley, its collection of half-timbered cottages and bright gardens made a charming picture, which could be seen from the sitting-room window of the rectory, a time-worn Jacobean structure perched near the church on a slight rise of ground.

Sophia often looked lovingly down on her beloved village before she started out on her customary visits to indigent cottagers. She hoped that she would never have to leave Oakley, even when the vicarage had a new tenant. She even knew precisely where she wanted to live. Down a pleasant lane on the other side of the settlement lay a tiny cottage which she and Miss Helver had earmarked for their own, if they ever set up house together in the future. The cottage belonged to the Oakley estate, and they would rent it from the marquis when the time came.

Sophia found it refreshing to pause in her round of visits and look in on the cottage, and this she did on the very morning after the day she had made her shocking bargain with the marquis. Basket over her arm, she stepped down the narrow lane, pausing once or twice to pluck some rosehips from the hedgerow. She was in need of solace, for somehow during the night she had gone from reasonable good cheer to a morbid sense that she had just made the greatest mistake of her life. Allow the marquis of Carrisbrooke to bed her? Had she taken leave of her senses?

Well, looking at the cottage would calm her grim thoughts today, as it always did, thought Sophia as she came in sight of her beloved dream. The tiny stone house was simply built and fronted by an overgrown garden of roses and lavender. Vines crept up all the walls in a most picturesque manner. Sophia had always loved the romantic look of this small structure, which had gone untenanted for as long as she could remember. Sometimes a workman from the Park would come and make some essential repair to the walls or the thatch, for it wouldn't do for his lordship's property to tumble down, but otherwise it was neglected. As a small girl Sophia had been used to creep away from the vicarage to come and play in the abandoned cottage, and she knew that behind the vine-covered walls were two rooms, one the kitchen, one a possible bedroom or sitting room. There was a large, finished attic upstairs which might also, with the proper alteration, serve as two small bedrooms.

Today Sophia walked all the way round the little place as she usually did, picking her way through the overgrown plants of the neglected garden and planning where she herself would one day plant the herbs, the vegetables, the flowers. Yet such homely thoughts helped but little to put the laughing face of Carrisbrooke out of her mind. Her anger at her own audacity grew until she was more than ready to escape the trap she'd set for herself. And in spite of his apparent readiness for dalliance, the marquis was a gentleman. He would never hold her to their bargain. Should she write him a note, begging him to forget what she had said? Should she beg him in person? She was just turning to head back up the lane and home when she heard a familiar voice call her name.

"Miss Dalrymple!"

An eager step heralded the arrival of Mr. Adolphus Penn, the Reverend Mr. Dalrymple's curate and the bane of Sophia's existence for five long years. An unprepossessing young man in whom a veneer of religious zeal unsuccessfully masked a self-serving nature, Mr. Penn, on first coming into the neighbourhood, had promptly selected the vicar's pretty daughter as the proper helpmeet for his self-sacrificing humble life—which in his private dreams included the eventual claiming of the living of Oakley, and then later a more prosperous one, and—who knew?—perhaps much more.

Miss Dalrymple's constant refusal of his suit was no deterrent to Mr. Penn. It was as plain as a pikestaff that she must eventually marry him or dwindle into an old maid, for how many men were unselfish and unworldly enough to saddle themselves with a penniless bride? Sophia's charming looks had initially attracted Penn, and the efficiency with which she helped her father had decided the curate in earnest to make her his wife. She would be the perfect minister's lady, and would even grace a bishopric if Penn's wilder dreams should come to pass.

"Good morning, sir," said Sophia in as cheerful a voice as she could manage. She often secretly deplored her father's lack of economy; and to her mind the most extravagant of Mr. Dalrymple's flights was, not his indiscriminate charity to neighbours, but his hiring of a curate. Whenever Sophia looked at Mr. Penn she saw fifty pounds a year. It was useless to remind herself that her papa really needed a curate's help at his age, and that Mr. Penn's advent had given the vicar precious time to spend in his library, which was his greatest joy. Sophia still resented Penn, though she knew she would not despise him quite so much if he would leave off insisting that she marry him.

The curate smiled. His slightly equine face and sturdy, graceless figure had always forcibly reminded Sophia of a workhorse, and she resisted the urge to give him one of the apples she had in her basket. As always when she met Mr. Penn, her mind next turned to the problem at hand: how to get away from him. He had come down this lane and she was just starting back up it, so this shouldn't be too difficult today—she hoped.

"Come to look at the cottage? I know it's a favourite spot of yours," said Penn, his own watery eyes briefly scanning the small enchanting place.

Sophia frowned. Penn seemed to soil her cottage merely by looking at it.

"Shall we turn around now? I'll conduct you to your next stop," the curate continued, oblivious to Sophia's black looks, or, perhaps, used to them.

Faced with such unwanted civility, Sophia was compelled to say that she had finished with that morning's calls and was on her way home. She had to accept Mr. Penn's escort along the leafy, sun-dappled roads to the vicarage, but how she wished that someone else were her companion instead. *Anyone* else! Her major fear now was that the curate might seize the opportunity for one of his declarations.

He did. "You must permit me, Miss Dalrymple," Penn said without any sort of preamble, as they walked along, "to renew those earnest solicitations for your hand to which, as you know, I must ever aspire." He then paused and waited politely.

Mr. Penn had been doing this for five years, at regular intervals, and in this time Sophia had trained him to the point where he no longer made awkward grasping motions in the direction of her person, nor fell upon his knees, nor even coloured his words with unnecessary passion. The only thing he wouldn't agree to do was to forget entirely the notion of marrying her.

"Dear sir," replied Sophia with the benign impersonal smile she used to accompany her refusals, "we've discussed this many times. I have no thoughts of marriage; I cannot leave my dear father. And you and I should never suit—you know I am convinced of that."

Of course Mr. Penn could not agree. The only thing about Miss Dalrymple which did not suit *him* was her portionless state, and this he had always been gallantly prepared to discount. He knew that under her professed reason of not wishing to leave her father must lurk a modest knowledge that she was really beneath the very eligible Adolphus Penn's notice. But he was not so mercenary a creature that he would give up such a beautiful, efficient bride, kind though it was of her to wish him a better-dowered helpmeet! Ignoring her statement, therefore, with all the chivalry he felt swelling his breast, he urged Sophia in several reasonable, oft-repeated sentences to reconsider her hasty decision and make him the happiest of men. As always, she refused with thanks and begged him not to open the subject again with her.

Then, this formality over, the talk could turn to other things, beginning with an account of all the tenants of Oakley whom Sophia had visited that morning. Old Dame Sykes' indisposition, the Browns' new baby and Billy Crow's broken leg were all discussed, Mr. Penn promising to visit these and other parishioners later in the day with his own peculiar brand of prosing suggestions for forbearance through faith.

"And now," he said when they were walking up the slight incline near the rectory, "I'll tell you the piece of news I learned just this morning at the Park. I've been saving it, for I know it will astonish you as it did me, dear Miss Dalrymple, and such a very strange thing could well overset you, in which case it is better to be near your home when I make the communication." He paused dramatically.

Sophia's eyebrows flew up, and she gazed at her companion in astonishment. "You've already overset me, Mr. Penn, but you must know I'm not a female given to the vapours. My word, has anything happened to Lady Amarantha or her daughter?"

"No, no, it isn't anything unpleasant," Mr. Penn assured her. "At least not unpleasant in the way you mean. The ladies at the Park are both in perfect health. What is astonishing is that Lady Amarantha's brother arrived yesterday. Sold out of the army, it seems."

If Penn had hoped to shock the lady, he was disappointed, for she merely gave a rather shaky laugh and said lightly, "Oh, that is old news, sir. Our Dolly is most diligent about picking up the latest on-dits, and she told me about the marquis's visit yesterday." Sophia didn't add that she had already encountered the notorious nobleman, but a little smile played about her lips as she let her thoughts wander off, considering what Mr. Penn would say if he could have witnessed the scene that had taken place between the proper Miss Dalrymple and the marquis of Carrisbrooke the day before.

Mr. Penn's voice recalled her to the present, and she shook her head and apologized for woolgathering. "If I may repeat myself, Miss Dalrymple," said the curate with a touch of injury apparent in his rather grating voice, "I don't wonder at your shock being even greater than my own. It can be no pleasant prospect for a gently bred lady such as yourself to be forced to be civil to such a libertine as we know Carrisbrooke to be. Not," added Mr. Penn in his own imitation of charity, "that I would ever be so harsh as to say such a thing of a fellow creature had I not heard of his reputation for years, and not thought him to be more pitied than scorned."

Sophia hid a smile. "It's very kind of you to make allowances for the marquis," she said, "for you must admit that we here in Hertfordshire have never had any but secondhand reports of his activities. Why, he may be no more of a libertine than yourself, sir."

There was a short silence as both Miss Dalrymple and her escort visualized the latter in the role of rake. Sophia struggled to control her laughter, and Mr. Penn his unchristian longings. By this time they had reached the wicket gate of the parsonage, and the curate took his leave.

Sophia stood and regarded the sturdy back of Mr. Penn as he moved in his stiff way toward the village High Street, where he lodged. Very soon he had passed out of sight, down the hill and round a turning in the road. But Sophia continued to stare in his direction, thinking over the offer of marriage he had just made her.

Penn's proposal had given her new confidence in her rash bargain with the marquis, and a new reality to her assertions that she had no plans to marry. There was really no comparison between Lord Carrisbrooke and Mr. Penn, but the thought of giving her virginity to the latter gentleman, under any condition, filled Sophia with nothing less than horror. Whereas the thought of descending into the shadowy world of sin with the marquis made the blood pound excitingly in her ears. This surely must mean that her decision was moral, in a twisted way.

It wasn't easy for a clergyman's daughter to justify an illicit liaison, but Sophia was doing her best.

CHAPTER FIVE

AMARANTHA SET DOWN the last sheet of copperplate script and neatened the substantial pile of manuscript pages on the table standing to one side of her velvet-covered chaise longue. Ringing for her maid, she asked that her brother be summoned to her boudoir.

In less than five minutes Carrisbrooke marched into the room, a commanding figure in evening dress of deep blue superfine coat and pearl-white pantaloons, Amarantha not being one of those sticklers who demanded that her gentlemen guests wear breeches for dinners in the country. His sister noticed fondly that his bearing was still quite military.

"What, not dressed yet?" he queried, casting an eye over Amarantha's lace-trimmed dressing robe and frivolous boudoir cap. "Your dinner guests are due in half an hour. Thought you wanted me to pick out your jewelry or some such thing." His glance strayed to the stack of papers on the table, and he grinned.

Smiling back at him, Amarantha replied, "It's entirely your fault, Charles, that I'm not dressed, for I've been veritably engrossed in this novel of Miss Dalrymple's. The girl's extraordinarily gifted. I find it so hard to reconcile this new image of an artist with the Miss Dalrymple I know: reserved, charitable, all of those tiresome things that clergymen's daughters always are."

Carrisbrooke couldn't help grinning even more broadly as he reconciled this image with that of the very untiresome Miss Dalrymple he had so unaccountably become acquainted with in the vicarage garden three days before.

Misinterpreting his expression, his sister said with a laugh, "Well, she *is* the most vexingly angelic creature, forever scampering about to cottages and organizing sales of work."

A snicker escaped the marquis. "And a novelist besides. Is she really a woman of no little talent, then? I suppose it's the usual run of spine-tingling tales. Shall I take it to the Minerva Press?"

"By no means, it isn't at all in that lurid style," protested Amarantha, wrinkling her brow in an attempt to find words to describe Miss Dalrymple's manuscript to someone who would likely never read a novel. "It's quite, quite real," she finally said in a moment of inspiration. "It's a simple domestic tale, about a girl who has problems getting married, and how she deals with her relations and friends. Miss Dalrymple has quite an eye for character; I'd swear some of her people must be drawn from life, and it's no wonder she wants to remain anonymous."

"Anonymous?"

"Yes, it says so on the first page. That style is quite the thing, I believe, for ladies of the ton who write *romans à clef* and want people to guess who they are, but it will also be convenient for a countrified female of retired habits such as Miss Dalrymple."

Carrisbrooke looked thoughtful. It was a new idea to him that the young author in question had actually offered her virtue in exchange for a publication that wouldn't bring her fame. Didn't people usually scribble novels in pursuit of notoriety? She must really be looking for nothing more than artistic recognition—and the resulting necessary income.

Amarantha was continuing, "She seems to have picked up quite an education somewhere. Of course her father is a very learned man, and she spent some time at school, that seminary where Helvie used to teach—Miss Helver, the governess, you know. But this knack for making words into real people must come to her naturally. I wouldn't hesitate a moment in taking the book to Murray, Charles."

"I certainly will, if you so suggest, and I'll tell him it was at your recommendation."

"Good. He's an excellent publisher and he knows I can judge these things. And now, I hope Sophia and her father get here tonight before those tiresome Hawthornes. I long to tell her how I like her book, and I wouldn't care to mention it before strangers, the dear young woman is so very modest." Amarantha got to her feet in a rustle of lace. "Now do go away, Charles. I positively must throw myself together."

Sophia. So that was the girl's Christian name, thought Carrisbrooke as he sauntered out of his sister's room. He smiled, remembering Amarantha's elevated idea of Miss Dalrymple's modesty and retiring nature. The vicar's daughter might possess such qualities; but far more interesting was the strange quirk of character that had led her to offer her person to a man she had never met before, and whom she couldn't fail to have heard described as a libertine.

His doubtful reputation with the ladies was probably the very reason she *had* chosen him as her intended patron, the marquis mused as he navigated the main staircase and directed his march toward the drawing room. He chuckled wickedly in a manner that would no doubt be approved by the young lady as a sign of his lack of morals, and thought with pleasure of the delicious irony of the situation. There could really be no doubt that his rakish habits had netted him this extraordinary prospective mistress: a parish angel, an organizer of sales of work! Quite a change from the usual selection he was wont to make from among the most dashing high-flyers on the Town— though it must be admitted that the adventurous wives of some of his associates had often been his prey as well, or he theirs.

Amarantha, a vision in a half-dress of figured amber silk, her chestnut hair done to perfection in a Sappho, entered the drawing room in a mere twenty-five minutes and beamed expectantly at her brother, who was leaning at his ease against the mantelpiece. "No one in England can dress with such speed, and to such effect," Carrisbrooke admitted with a bow and a half-mocking smile.

"I know that," said Amarantha with becoming modesty. "Now where is Echo? She ought to be here, for the vicar is always punctual, and he and Sophia should be arriving at any moment."

"I believe my niece went to root out a dish of sugared walnuts she mentioned seeing in the morning room. She passed through here a moment ago," answered Carrisbrooke with a grin. "Not the fluttering state of nerves you'd expect from a young girl in her situation."

For this was a special evening for Echo. Amarantha rarely entertained in the country, and she had conceived of this party as the perfect occasion for young Echo to dine in company for the first time. The girl, yawning at the very thought of being catapulted into the mysterious world of adults, had been summarily stuffed into a white muslin evening gown, and her hair done up in a new, becoming style, in anticipation of this meeting with the Dalrymples and the Hawthorne family, the Burroughses' nearest neighbours. Carrisbrooke had barely had time to notice Echo's transformed appearance as his niece made her casual pass through the drawing room in search of sustenance. And he had certainly not remarked any nervous fluttering.

Amarantha sighed over her wayward daughter's appetite and sat down. When Echo—and the dish of walnuts—appeared a moment or two later, her mother said a stern word or two on the subject of ladies and their delicate appetites, to which Echo calmly attended between bites.

"Let the child keep her little eccentricities—she'll be an original," advised Echo's uncle from his place by the fire. His eyes twinkled conspiratorially at his niece. "Pretty as she is, she'll not lack for admirers, not even if she devours a saddle of lamb singlehanded at the highest table in the land."

"She's perfectly capable of that," sighed Amarantha. She eyed her passively grazing daughter with something akin to envy; Lady Amarantha had to take every care to maintain her own stately figure, and it was vexing to have given birth to a wandlike creature of fairy-tale beauty who incidentally never stopped eating.

"Miss Dalrymple said the same as Uncle Charles, and she is very wise," was Echo's contribution to the discussion, uttered in a thoughtful voice. Then, lifting her wide blue eyes to the marquis's face, she added, "Uncle, I shall marry a man just like you."

"That's the spirit I like to see," Amarantha said with a laugh. "See that you do keep yourself fixed to that goal, child. Bring home a marquis."

"And a handsome devil," added the irrepressible Carrisbrooke.

"I shall try," said Echo. She returned to her interrupted task, and set down the empty walnut dish just in time to greet the party from the vicarage.

When the Dalrymples were announced, Sophia, hovering with her father behind the Burroughs butler, felt an almost overpowering urge to turn and run out of the house. Not only was she facing Lady Amarantha for the first time since that lady had presumably been let into the secret of her novel writing; this was daunting enough. She was also to meet her prospective seducer for the first time since their disturbing embrace in the woods.

Sophia had done nothing but think about this evening with alternating dread and anticipation ever since Lady Amarantha's invitation had arrived at the vicarage the day before. She had guessed that the lady was reading the novel and would wish to talk to her about it, and she had accordingly had no choice but to tell her father about the marquis's proposed patronage, leaving out the most important detail of the agreement. Papa had been immediately congratulatory, and flattered that she had followed his advice. He had praised Sophia's courage as well as the talent which would no doubt carry her on to fortune with the marquis's push, without which she would never get her foot in the door of the publishing world.

Many a thought on the frivolous subject of her wardrobe had busied Sophia's mind as she had anticipated this party. She was a person who relied heavily on costume to fix herself properly in the role she had to play; thus every stitch she owned loudly announced the clergyman's daughter of mature years. She had nothing that would show her to Carrisbrooke in a seductive, dashing light—not that it was necessary to do such a thing now, to be sure. His "bargain" with her had already been struck, and it was obviously not contingent upon her clothing, for he had made it when she had been wearing her oldest dress, with her hair all undone. Nevertheless, as she put herself into the severely styled blue silk gown she had worn on every formal occasion in the past two years, Sophia couldn't help mentally designing an absolutely stunning toilette that would be perfect for a Cyprian: diaphanous white and silver gauze, perhaps, cut extremely low, worn with one damped petticoat, and fastened down the front with silver acorns. Sophia tried to imagine herself in such a gown as she made her greetings to the company.

Carrisbrooke was secretly amused by the extreme change in this prim Miss Dalrymple in blue, her curly black hair bound up in a severe style, from the seductively clothed, abandoned creature whom he had recently kissed. (He couldn't know that, far from being a costume chosen for its sensual appeal, the gown she'd been wearing that day had clung indecently to her figure because the fabric was so old and soft.) He bowed gravely over the hand of the proper-looking lady before him tonight and received as serious a curtsey in return. Then as he straightened he looked her in the eye and winked.

She positively jumped and seemed about to make some reply when she was summoned by Amarantha. The two ladies soon had their heads together in one corner of the room.

This left Carrisbrooke to talk to the vicar. Mr. Dalrymple immediately tendered his thanks on his daughter's behalf, praising the marquis's kind intended patronage of the dear child's work. While responding affably to these comments and discounting his own part in the scheme as very minor indeed, Carrisbrooke let his glance stray to Sophia. The lady was looking pleased and flattered; no doubt Amarantha was praising her work with the same enthusiasm Mr. Dalrymple was giving to his laudatory remarks about Carrisbrooke's kindness.

Echo, as befitted a young girl, sat by silently and audited both conversations. It was news to her that Miss Dalrymple wrote, but she didn't look surprised. To Echo, there was not much difference between reading books and writing them. She supposed someone had to do the latter.

The Hawthornes, Sir Robert and his lady and their two adolescent sons, arrived before too long. The boys gravitated at once toward the lovely Miss Burroughs, overloading her with compliments and attentions.

And then a very curious thing took place. Echo sprang suddenly from her torpor into sparkling life, laughing and flirting quite as if she were well practiced. Her mama, having foreseen this, applauded her own insight, reflecting sagely that a lively daughter might be a blessing as well as a curse the following spring.

But Amarantha had no time to meditate further on Echo's behaviour with the young men. Lady Hawthorne had sailed over to her hostess and Miss Dalrymple, and she now regaled them with an anecdote about Sir Robert's last bilious attack; and Sir Robert, all unknowing that such an intimate facet of his personal life was being set forth for the entertainment of the ladies present, joined the marquis and the vicar and companionably discussed London life with the former, completely excluding the country clergyman.

Dinner proceeded in this style. The marquis had to hand in Lady Hawthorne, in the natural course of things, and was thus unable to direct more than a look or two Sophia's way. The Hawthornes were the sort of family who had no qualms about monopolizing the general conversation with their own concerns, and they matter-of-factly did so. In truth Sir Robert and Lady Hawthorne were the only ones guilty of this, for their sons, sparring rather clumsily for the favour of the beautiful Echo, could not be said to be conversing at all. But though the Hawthornes might be tedious, they were also the only close neighbours of gentility that Oakley Park could boast, and Lady Amarantha appreciated them as such. She appreciated them even more when they had to leave soon after the tea was served, owing to the distance of their home from Oakley.

"I'm so glad to have a chance to be more private with you and your father, dear," said Lady Amarantha to Miss Dalrymple as soon as the wheels of the Hawthorne carriage could be heard retreating into the distance. "I have the most wonderful idea."

Sophia looked up expectantly, and the marquis, who was observing her, was struck once more by the brilliance of her eyes.

"Now see if you don't all think this is splendid," continued Amarantha, turning to include the vicar and her brother in her conversation. Echo, meanwhile, was across the room, strumming on the pianoforte, whereon reposed a dish of biscuits snatched from the tea cart. "We know it probably takes a long time to get novels all printed and bound."

"Quite probably, sister. And?" prodded the marquis.

"Well, it's late summer now. It might be as far away as spring before Sophia's novel can be published. And my idea is that she travel with Echo and me when we go to Town for the season. Only think, my dear—" she smiled at Sophia and pressed her hand "—you would be in London to see how your book takes. Wouldn't you like that?"

Sophia, looking most disturbed, began to voice objections which featured her inability to leave her father's side, her lack of means to afford such a trip and a dozen other obstacles.

"Oh, my dear, of course you'd go as our guest, and for as short a time as you like. No need to worry about Mr. Dalrymple," Amarantha said, tossing off the problems one by one. "Isn't that right, sir?" she appealed to the vicar.

That worthy gentleman was obliged to say that he could manage without Sophia very well, should she care to take part in such a scheme.

The marquis took it upon himself to urge Miss Dalrymple to go, and she blushed painfully. Lady Amarantha added the offer of a servant or two from the Park to care for the vicar's comfort and make parish visits during Sophia's absence. Finally even Echo, hearing the discussion, added her urgings that Miss Dalrymple go, as it would be "such fun."

Sophia was secretly alarmed at the thought of going anywhere as the guest of the relations of the man who would someday be relieving her of her virginity, but she was also undeniably excited by the thought of seeing the metropolis for the first time, being on the spot when her book appeared—if it were really going to!—and observing at close range a young lady's come-out. It would be a marvellous experience for her writing! She wouldn't allow herself to accept Lady Amarantha's invitation at once, however; she knew that the decision to leave her father must be thought out carefully, for she had never been away from him since the death of her mother and could only imagine the extra work her absence would create. She finally promised to think over the matter seriously, adding that it was such a long time till spring that quite a few things could change by then.

"But some things won't," said Carrisbrooke loudly. Everyone but a chagrined Sophia was mystified by this seemingly philosophical comment, and the talk moved on at last to other subjects.

Excusing herself as soon as the company's attention was directed away from her, Sophia rose from her seat and took a turn or two about the room to calm herself. However, as the marquis was watching her every move with an infuriating twinkle in his attractive brown eyes, this operation was almost totally inefficacious.

"Miss Dalrymple, if you've a mind to be strolling about, let me show you the pottery shards my great-uncle brought back from Italy," Carrisbrooke proposed, getting up from his chair. "They're over in the corner in a cabinet.'' He flashed Sophia a meaning, intimate smile as he fell into step beside her and took her arm. It was an excellent time to snatch a semiprivate interview, Sophia noted. The vicar was busily describing to Lady Amarantha some of his latest activities in the service of Oakley parish, and Echo had returned to the piano, where she was regaling the company with a very indifferent version of ''Robin Adair.'' Sophia allowed herself to be steered toward the japanned cupboard in question and stared at the shards which nestled within on glass shelves, each chip of pottery with its own unintelligible label.

''Great-uncle was the veriest bore on the subject of his archaeology,'' said Carrisbrooke loudly, ''but one must admit he made some important discoveries, and the subject is fascinating, ma'am, if explained by the right person.''

''And you are the right person, my lord?'' asked Sophia, with a smile at her companion. Then, realizing that she'd given him an opening to allude to their future, she hoped he would take her words in a light, joking spirit.

''So you have indicated,'' replied the marquis in a low voice.

Sophia turned crimson. ''My dear sir, there's no reason to tease me with talk of our bargain until the time is nearer for it to be, er, fulfilled,'' she whispered in great distress. ''You may be sure I won't come to London if you'll be there.''

Carrisbrooke drew himself up to his full height. ''My dear Miss Dalrymple,'' he said with dignity, ''I can't direct your movements, of course. But you are, in a manner of speaking, my responsibility from now on, a choice I will not hesitate to remind you that you made yourself. Please don't try to limit the ways in which I reap the fruits of my—labours on your behalf." He glanced about the room, seemed to see a clear field, then leaned down quickly to kiss Sophia on the lips. His arm, which had been innocently crooked to allow her hand to nestle within it, reached out for the merest second to clasp and caress her waist. Then he was the proper, formal nobleman once more.

As she listened to a surprisingly knowledgeable lecture on the fascinating discoveries at Pompeii, Sophia wondered bleakly what she had got herself into.

CHAPTER SIX

"LITTLE BROTHER CHARLES," wrote Lady Amarantha Burroughs one day the following spring—for she thoroughly took advantage of the fact that she was the only person in the world who could so style the marquis of Carrisbrooke—

I hope this finds you well and over your latest scrape involving the Italian singer. She sounds what you would call a prime bit, and you are not to spread it about the Town that I use such language! Echo and I will be in London before you know it, next week to be exact. I am delighted to accept your invitation to open Carrisbrooke House for the season, and I warn you that you'll find yourself obliged to give your niece a come-out ball. Worry only about the expense, dear brother; the trouble I engage to take on myself. How goes Miss Dalrymple's book? I so long to see it. I have been wearing down the girl's resolve all the winter, and she's finally agreed to journey up to Town with us and make what she will persist in calling a short visit. Naturally I couldn't hope to make the trip really worthwhile for her by finding her a husband; as she points out, her age and situation quite preclude that. But she is an engaging creature once you get to know her and will be delightful to have in the house. I do pine for rational companionship in the domestic circle—not to denigrate you, dear Charles, but you will be so rarely at your sister's disposal...

Carrisbrooke looked up from his sister's missive, and his eyes held a familiar amused gleam that hadn't been there in months. It did his sense of mischief a world of good to hear that the Oakley party would be arriving in London almost at once, and that Sophia would indeed be with the ladies. It was an age since he had seen Miss Dalrymple—Christmas week, in fact, when he had gone up to pass the holiday with his sister and niece and had managed to corner the vicar's daughter as she decorated the church, and to maul her about in a way that he, for one, had found almost too exciting. She had been her usual embarrassed, outraged self, but she'd responded. Ah, she had indeed responded. He chuckled.

The previous summer, on ending his visit to Hertfordshire, Carrisbrooke had journeyed directly to London and laid Miss Dalrymple's manuscript on the very desk of John Murray, Esq., of Albemarle Street: the great Murray, who had been called the only gentleman in the publishing business, and whose clients included Scott and Byron. Carrisbrooke was acquainted with the esteemed publisher already, for they had met after his archaeologist great-uncle's death to discuss the disposition of his uncle's instructive book on Greek statuary. Mr. Murray, intrigued by the thought of the most unliterary Carrisbrooke patronizing an anonymous lady, had promised to read the novel with a kind eye.

Swinging his sister's letter back and forth in a way that would have struck that lady as characteristically disrespectful, Carrisbrooke thought back to the interview that had taken place in Mr. Murray's office the following week.

"WHO WROTE THIS?" the publisher asked frankly, tapping the manuscript and favouring his noble guest with a shrewd look.

The marquis shrugged. He had already explained that the lady preferred to remain anonymous.

"It wasn't Lady Amarantha Burroughs, by any chance?" was Murray's next statement. "Always thought she had a head on her shoulders, and an eye for character."

Carrisbrooke started. "Why, no, as it happens, it wasn't. My sister is the one who read it, though. It's here at her recommendation."

"Not your own? You haven't read it, my lord?"

Amazed at this line of questioning, Carrisbrooke answered shortly, "No."

Murray leaned back in his chair. "I only ask, Lord Carrisbrooke, because it would seem that whoever did write this book knows you very well. You appear in it, sir. As . . . as the hero."

His noble guest considered this. Carrisbrooke knew that Murray had just made an impossible statement, for Sophia Dalrymple had written the book before he and she had ever met. And to his knowledge she had never even seen him from afar. He decided, however, to be inscrutable on this issue. "Indeed?" he said in his best indolent, bored manner, looking as though he belonged in the bow window at White's and not on the other side of John Murray's desk.

The other man nodded and smiled in professional anticipation. "She's got you to the life! With yourself a character in the book, and known to be its patron, well, sir, it's bound to sell, especially if I delay its appearance till the start of next season, to catch all the notables in Town."

Carrisbrooke inclined his head, still putting on the pose of bored sophisticate. "How fortunate."

"Much as I want to publish this, it's only fair to give you every chance to reconsider the move," said Murray next. "You aren't presented in any bad light, to be sure, but it might be misconstrued as an invasion of your privacy. Why not read it and get back to me?"

At this point the marquis considered that he had to know more. "Just how am I portrayed, then?" he asked curiously. "What leads you to think the character is based on me?"

Murray shrugged. "Physical type similar. Situation in life not equal, but similar—she makes you an earl. The plot, well, the plot is, I must admit, an out-and-out fabrication. These small similarities of looks and manner would possibly not be regarded, but you know how the ton hunts these anonymous novels for likenesses. And with you the work's patron..."

Carrisbrooke laughed. "It's simple to stop that. Don't put it about that I've anything to do with the book, and I'll scrape by. Must be the merest coincidence that I'm, er, recognizable, by the way. I happen to know that the authoress has never met me. Not till the book was written, shall I say."

The interview was soon concluded, and Murray, looking slightly disappointed that his "puffing" of the novel wouldn't include a reference to Carrisbrooke, did assure the marquis that the book could stand on its own merit and secretly vowed to let word slip out as if by hazard that the handsome nobleman was somehow concerned. Months would have to pass before this could occur, and Carrisbrooke would forget all about his careless patronage. Why, it was clear that he wasn't interested even now in reading the thing, not even to see how he had been fictionalized!

Murray hadn't even really begun to consider that the resemblance he had noticed might be coincidental. Would the personification of a novel's hero bring it in to be published and have nothing to do with its creation? No, that was doing it a bit too brown. But as the marquis's insistence had seemed sincere, the publisher did spend some thoughtful moments in trying to tie the character he had recognized as Lord Carrisbrooke to some other notable in society. It was just possible that the authoress had had another peer in her mind, and that the marquis's patronage had caused one to jump to the conclusion that it was he. The publisher ruminated along these lines for a full five minutes before returning to his first opinion—that the marquis of Carrisbrooke was assisting his own character into novel form, for whatever fanciful reason.

The marquis of Carrisbrooke, momentarily diverted by the thought that Sophia had accidentally described a person who might be thought to resemble himself, came to his own conclusion: that John Murray, Esq., was so used to reading the novelized confessions of ladies of fashion that he couldn't conceive of a writer of the gentler sex relying upon creativity rather than real life when populating a novel. Sophia must simply have worked from her imagination only; she lived retired in the country and knew no earls, and as Carrisbrooke had pointed out to Murray, had never even met him until the manuscript was completed. A further proof that Murray was chasing moonbeams was the fact that Amarantha, who would certainly be the first to recognize a fictionalized Carrisbrooke, had mentioned nothing of the sort. It never occurred to the marquis that his sister might have had her own reasons for not remarking on such a resemblance.

AS CARRISBROOKE CHUCKLED over the letter from his sister months later, a mere four weeks before the scheduled appearance of Sophia's book, he amused himself by mulling over whether it would be advisable to move from these comfortable and snug bachelor quarters in the Albany to take up his abode in immense, draughty Carrisbrooke House with the ladies. It would certainly be proper; in fact, it might be the only respectable thing to do, considering that the marquis in residence elsewhere in London than his opened house would give rise to speculation—and it would drive Sophia into Bedlam. Yes, he would certainly do it!

Carrisbrooke's winter had been filled with a wealth of activities. He had made the rounds of all his holdings, initiating the new farming techniques he had studied; he had haunted livestock auctions and the stables of noted horse and cattle breeders in search of animals; he had set in motion several repairs to his various houses, and planned new, modern cottages of his own design for some of his tenants.

These innocent and worthy bucolic activities had been offset by several healthy doses of Town life. The marquis had traded stories with his army friends at the clubs, discussed the issues of the day with the most

noted politicians in preparation for taking his seat in
the House, and despite a new lack of real interest in
the demimonde, he'd been conspicuous in his petticoat dealings, as Amarantha had seen fit to mention
in her letter. But though he had been busy and had
accomplished much, his life had lacked a certain vi-
tality which he could sense returning now.

Carrisbrooke rang for his secretary, Mr. Mudgely,
a very shrewd and efficient young man who read law
in what moments he could snatch from tending to the
marquis's concerns, and was soon dictating various
orders which dealt with the formal opening of Carrisbrooke House in Grosvenor Square.

The very correct and notoriously observant Mr.
Mudgely had a momentary stab of something like
disappointment; for he had been as happy as his master in this tonnish haven of masculinity where they had
their chambers. But he had soon brought himself
round to the proper enthusiasm for what was, really,
a great event. A secretary's consequence could only be
helped if he and his employer moved to one of the
great mansions of the Town.

On the other hand, such worldly considerations as
Mudgely had to admit he felt could hardly be shared
by Carrisbrooke, who was already a marquis. Try as
he would, Mudgely couldn't bring himself to understand the inordinate pleasure his master appeared to
take in what any young, unattached nobleman would
naturally regard as a crashing bore and a dismal ne-
cesssity: namely, the setting up of a sister and niece in
one's house, the prospective move of oneself to that

very feminine fortress and the promise of forced attendance as escort at dozens of banal, insipid social activities, all suitable for a young lady in her first season.

CHAPTER SEVEN

MISS SOPHIA DALRYMPLE descended from the crested coach of the marquis of Carrisbrooke and followed his sister and niece up the steps and through the stern, forbidding portals of the house in Grosvenor Square. It was early evening, and London was beginning to bustle, after a late-afternoon pause, with the myriad activities of the Town after dark. The gas street lamps had just been lit and cast a warm yellow glow over the vast square and the elegant buildings that lined it.

Sophia, who had never been to London in all her four and twenty years, was already glad that a combination of her father's insistence and Lady Amarantha's bullying had finally pushed her to the point of accepting her ladyship's invitation. For no matter what indignities the mischievous marquis might inflict upon her—and she did not at all trust that maddening, quizzing face, for all its handsomeness, and for all the man's insistence that by deviling her with his attentions he was only keeping to their "bargain"—she could tell that the experience of being in the metropolis would do her the world of good. It would help her writing as well as her personal education. She had already been astonished by the great amount of traffic and by the sheer expanse of the London streets. She could only imagine how great would be the variety of people she might meet here, even though she hardly intended to go out into society.

Lady Amarantha was also happy to be in Town. The Hertfordshire winter, never her favorite experience, had nearly been the death of her this year, so anxious was she to bring her daughter out and see Miss Dalrymple's novel in print, both of which events must take place in Town. How generous it had been of Charles to open Carrisbrooke House! Not that he had been given much choice in the matter. His sister cast an approving glance round the large parqueted hall of Carrisbrooke House, with its highly polished Sheraton furnishings, before shrugging off her cloak into the arms of her attendant dresser and motioning her daughter and Miss Dalrymple to follow her up the stairs.

"We'll sit in the drawing room, my dears—the smaller one—and catch our breath," she was saying as she sailed into the salon in question. "Then, according to Charles, there'll be a late dinner waiting for us, and we can begin to plot our strategies for our tour of the shops tomorrow."

"Indeed you can," said a familiar deep voice, and the ladies all started violently as the marquis unfolded his long frame from a sofa in the corner. He was flawless in sober evening dress, from the sleek fit of his corbeau-coloured coat to the high shine on his pumps, and Sophia, caught off her guard and gazing raptly, thought that she had never seen the man looking so handsome. The immaculate simplicity of his attire acted as a superb frame for his classical good looks, crop of chestnut hair and powerful figure. His brown eyes held an amused, intimate expression as he bowed formally in Sophia's direction after a more effusive flurry of hugs and kisses initiated by his sister and niece.

"And you're really remaining in tonight to dine with us, brother," Amarantha enthused as the group took seats in a circle of Louis Quatorze chairs upholstered in straw-coloured satin. A sly glance followed this statement. "Is it solely for our benefit, or have you done something delightfully scandalous again, and find it easier to spend an evening *en famille* so the talk can die down?"

"Purely my brotherly affection coming to the fore, sister, I assure you," drawled Carrisbrooke with a negligent shrug. But his eyes lit on Miss Dalrymple for just an instant, long enough to arouse his sister's secret amusement and to make Sophia blush.

Echo had already risen from her seat to flit about the room in her usual birdlike manner, which those who knew her best could recognize as a systematic search for the bon-bon dishes which might lurk in any strange room. "We're so glad to be in Town at last, Uncle," she said with her dazzling smile, as she moved about. "Mama and I have been studying *La Belle Assemblée* all the winter, and I'm suffering for new clothes. And of course my come-out ball will be so thrilling. Will you show me the ballroom now?"

"Later, child," put in her mother. "Yes, Charles, Echo has discovered a new interest in finery since she's going to be a young lady, though I've warned her that the sprig muslins of the schoolroom set are remarkably little different from the things she'll be wearing as a debutante."

"Oh, but Mama, we've discussed how those little elegant touches by the first modistes can make all the difference," said Echo with an air of practised au-

thority that astonished the others. She had stood still
for this important pronouncement, but now resumed
her prowling of the gilt-and-straw environs, pausing
once before a mirror to survey with complacency her
blonde curls and Dresden-shepherdess face.

"And are you also planning to cut a swath through
the mantua-makers of the metropolis, Miss Dalrymple?" queried Carrisbrooke in his most pleasant, if
alliterative, manner.

Sophia turned even redder than his caressing glance
of a moment ago had made her; and because her de-
plorable tendency to blush in front of the marquis
vexed her terribly, she answered with more sharpness
than the question warranted. "Of course not, my lord.
You might recall that I'm quite the impecunious
country woman."

"I've been trying and trying to get her to accept a
few things as a gift from me," Amarantha put in with
a devilish smile; she had more than half guessed by
then that her brother had a devastating effect upon the
vicar's daughter. "But she simply refuses, though she
has consented to look at a few of my own gowns and
alter them for herself. You know how prone I am to
make grievous colour errors, Charles. There are a
dozen costumes I ought never to wear, and Sophia is
such a clever seamstress."

Carrisbrooke nodded seriously. He knew that
Amarantha's last mistake in fashion judgement had
occurred in her tenth year, when she had stolen a pair
of breeches from a stable lad to facilitate her riding
astride, and then been caught out by their mother. So
if Amarantha's substantial stock of clothes did include some which would be unbecoming to her lush
colouring and chestnut hair, then they must have been

put there on purpose to fit out Sophia. "No need for that," he said nevertheless, hoping to tease his lovely self-styled mistress to the utmost, "I quite understand that Miss Dalrymple's pride wouldn't allow her to accept gifts from us...."

Here a few choking sounds of protest broke from Sophia, who was aghast to hear how ungratefully stiff and puritanical his voicing of her reasons sounded.

The marquis continued without seeming to notice. "She can have no possible objection, though, to accepting a loan from me, to be repaid by the proceeds of the sale of her novel."

To her horror, Sophia's unbecoming sharpness was in evidence once more, as she replied almost without thinking, "Your lordship must realize that I won't be able to use up my income—if indeed I end having one—in such a frivolous way."

"Ah, yes, saving for your old age, wasn't it?" the marquis responded in good humour. "Well, we'll think of ways and means." He winked at his sister, then added as if in afterthought, "You haven't much need for a London modiste in any case, Miss Dalrymple. That costume you have on, to take but one example, does not disguise your charms in the least." He ran an appreciative eye over the garment in question.

Sophia couldn't help smiling with pleasure, and reflecting on how volatile her host's manners could be—mercilessly teasing one moment, gallant the next. She was indeed rather proud of her neat dark blue merino travelling costume, for she'd designed and made it herself, but she also knew it wouldn't hold up to tonnish London standards, and she made haste to say so. "But that's perfectly fine with me," she added serenely, "for I haven't come to Town to dazzle all and sundry with my fashion sense, but to remain quietly in the background and see my novel in the shops.''

Carrisbrooke and Lady Amarantha nodded gravely at this; Echo stared in surprise. The company then soon dispersed, and the ladies went off to their rooms to change for dinner.

Sophia was led to a spacious bedroom papered in white and silver, with light blue hangings and a wealth of elegant Queen Anne furniture. A housemaid was just finishing the unpacking of Miss Dalrymple's trunk and bandbox, and bowed herself out after Sophia had assured the girl that she needed no assistance in dressing. In fact, since she had seen to her own needs all her life, it shocked her more than a little to be waited on. But it occurred to her that the accoutrements of wealth did have their charms. Papa would no doubt have given a lecture on the dangers of luxurious living could he have known what his daughter was thinking.

For when she had been left alone, Sophia couldn't help exclaiming a little to herself in honest delight; she'd never slept in such a large, richly appointed room before. She hated to admit it, but she seemed to have an appreciation of luxury that would no doubt be most inconvenient in the years to come, especially those which would take place within the minuscule rooms of the cottage at Oakley village. But, she reminded herself sternly, interior space was as nothing when compared to the beauties of nature, and she had those in Hertfordshire. In London, where such vistas of countryside were not to be had, perhaps it was natural to delight in uncramped living quarters.

It took hardly any time at all for Sophia to wash, do her hair and array herself in her familiar blue silk gown, sadly crushed by the trip—it didn't occur to her that she might have asked the maid to press the costume for her—but the only decent thing she had to wear to dinner. When she was ready, but judged it too soon to venture into the drawing room—for she knew Echo and Lady Amarantha would likely still be busy under the ministrations of their dressers, and she had no desire to blunder into a tête-à-tête with Carrisbrooke—she sat down by the bedroom fire and essayed a moment of serious thinking.

She had known beforehand that the marquis would be resident in Grosvenor Square during her stay. Lady Amarantha had told her so, praising her brother's goodwill for putting himself to the trouble of moving when everyone knew how comfortable he was in his bachelor lodgings. But Sophia had somehow not considered before what his lordship's residence might mean. He could be staying in the house for, well, convenience. Perhaps he intended to claim her favours in this very room! She looked around nervously at the bedchamber at this point in her mental wanderings, expecting the surrounding shadows to take on a sinister aspect. Her book would be out in less than a month, and she was due to "pay" when that event occurred.

It must be said that in the many months following her strange pact with the marquis, Sophia had ceased to think of their agreement as serious. What gentleman could have taken her rather wild proposition to heart? She had more than half decided that Carrisbrooke was only teasing her, could not mean to seduce her, and would surprise her by revealing these chivalrous intentions soon. Such logical thinking had relieved her mind considerably, but she had to admit to a vague feeling of disappointment, and a small inner voice which demanded that *she* arrange the seduction, whatever her seducer's intentions. When one was this close to being Carrisbrooke's lover, why allow him to be gallant? the voice would whisper from time to time, especially when Sophia lay worrying in her bed at night. This particular inner voice was oblivious to such reasons as respectability, morality or even safety, for the idea of the bastard child, planted in Sophia's mind by Carrisbrooke himself, had been preying on her a good deal of late. Much as the vicar's daughter disdained to admit it, these shocking thoughts were motivated by her own surprising lust, and...and something else, which Sophia had no mind to identify as yet.

But it might be that Carrisbrooke did not intend to be chivalrous at all, that he was staying in the house for convenience during their proposed affair and would initiate said intrigue very soon. And what would she do if things really came to the point? Beg him to spare her, probably. With such thoughts alternately raising and depressing her spirits, the sedate-appearing Miss Dalrymple finally ventured down to dinner.

IN THE FOLLOWING DAYS the marquis was not much in evidence as the Burroughs ladies flitted from milliner to modiste, for Amarantha and especially Echo needed a complete fitting out before they could begin to accept invitations. Sophia shared vicariously in most of these outings into the exciting shopping streets of Town, her dressmaker's eye sharp as she tried to pick up the latest trends in cut and trim for the refurbishing of her own wardrobe. She was enjoying her-

self, she was sure, quite as much as she would have if
she'd had money to spend.

When she stayed in, which was fairly often, Sophia
wrote voluminous letters to her father and Miss Helver. She hadn't been separated from her father for five
years, and found that she missed him sorely. As for
Helvie, the governess had undertaken to make Sophia's parish rounds during her absence and, having
already come to cuffs once with the odious Mr. Penn,
needed much in the way of comfort and advice. Sophia also read, a luxury she didn't have much time in
which to indulge at home, and made copious notes for
a fourth novel. She was astonished by the number of
hours at her disposal: when one wasn't constantly occupied with domestic activities and didn't have the
fashionable habit of sleeping late, there was all the
time in the world to do whatever one wished!

She could move about the house in Grosvenor
Square without fear of meeting the marquis; he was
always out during the day, and only occasionally
joined his womenfolk in the evening.

Sophia told herself that this distance Carrisbrooke
was keeping from the ladies was for her own comfort;
for it must be obvious to the gentleman how nervous
he made her, and how much the thought of their
coming "association" distressed her. She knew she
ought to be grateful for his thoughtfulness.

However, she found to her vexation that she missed
him very much when he wasn't there, and looked up
expectantly every time a door opened in the house,
half hoping, half fearing to see a certain handsome,
mocking face.

CHAPTER EIGHT

BY COINCIDENCE Echo's come-out ball was scheduled in the very week that Sophia's novel was to appear, and preparations for what the marquis called
their "joint debut" were proceeding rapidly. Echo's
gauzy white gown was under construction at the house
of Fanchon; Lady Amarantha had sent cards of invitation to all and sundry, and had heard a gratifying
rumour that Prinny was planning to look in; and
Gunter's of Berkeley Square was to provide the supper which, at Echo's insistence, would include a
quantity of the delicate ices for which the confection-
ers' firm was justly famous.

On the day of the ball, Sophia, in the interests of
"collecting material," made several trips to the state
rooms of Carrisbrooke House, enjoying the exciting
atmosphere of an important night to come as servants gave the dance floor a final polish, set chairs for
the musicians in the gallery and placed flower arrangements at strategic points in the white and gilt
ballroom with its discreet alcoves and antechambers.
Never had she seen such festive bustle on such a large
scale.

After much discussion, Sophia had given in to
Amarantha's insistence that she attend the ball—but
only if she could do so unobtrusively. Amarantha had
agreed to set her guest free from the duty of playing a

part in the reception line, which Sophia claimed should never have been in the question anyway, since she was not a relation. In return for remaining in the background, Sophia had had to promise to dance whenever she was asked. Guessing that an unknown lady not in her first youth wouldn't be solicited for the dance in any case, Sophia had fallen in with this plan cheerfully enough and retired to dress on the evening of the ball in quite an excited mood, she judged, for one of her mature years.

Her dress, a gift from Lady Amarantha, was a pleasure to put on. It consisted of a rose-coloured satin underdress beneath an open robe of silver gauze. The overdress was fastened across the low-cut bodice with silver rosettes; and Amarantha had insisted on also giving Sophia a pair of silver slippers which she said pinched her own feet. They fit Miss Dalrymple's to a nicety and added an elegant, finished touch to the outfit. Sophia had given this ensemble a satisfied glance in the mirror, and was about to start on her hair when she heard a scratching at the door. It proved to be none other than Lady Amarantha's haughty dresser, Ross, come to beg Miss to go to her lady-ship's own chamber to put the finishing touches to her toilette and have her hair done. Touched by this attention, Sophia picked up her gloves and a painted fan that had belonged to her mother and hurried out into the hall after the abigail.

And there, coming down the corridor from the opposite direction, was the marquis, still in his day clothes. "Original style of hairdressing, ma'am," was the gentleman's impish comment as his eyes raked Sophia's costume.

Her heart pounding in a most distressing way, Sophia managed to nod impersonally, tossed the long unbound mane in question and allowed herself a half smile before proceeding to Lady Amarantha's boudoir.

"Magnificent, my dear," was Lady Amarantha's comment as she turned from her dressing table. She was in the act of clasping a fine necklace of emeralds around her white throat; her gown of pomona-green satin with gold floss trim was very effective, combining a fashionable seductiveness with what her ladyship laughingly called "a mere touch of the dowager" suitable for the mama of a grown girl. "Wasn't I right to give you that gown?" Lady Amarantha went on, her dark eyes dancing. "I really looked a quiz in that shade of pink, with such a red cast to my hair—cannot think what possessed me. But it is perfectly exquisite on you, Sophia. Now come let Ross do your hair. I long to see it *à la Meduse*."

Sophia obediently sat down while Lady Amarantha hovered and fussed over the details of her own appearance in the same mirror, and the former was startled at the finished effect of the new hairstyle. With her limited knowledge of fashion, she didn't know that the Meduse was scorned by many as too demimondaine; nor that Lady Amarantha and her dresser had spent a serious hour in discussing which arrangement would transform Miss Dalrymple into a *nonpareil*, finally deciding to modify the Meduse just a bit away from the demimonde. The result was an original style: a tantalizing, softly waved knot with escaping tendrils that blended with the shorter, curling hair around Sophia's face and gave her a new air of worldliness and distinction which caught the mood of her flattering, expensive gown.

"Ravishing," was Lady Amarantha's comment, uttered to the ladies' joint reflection in her largest cheval glass.

Sophia was more discerning than her ladyship believed her to be, and she had an idea that her becoming costume had never been intended for anyone other than herself. Impulsively she gave Amarantha a hug, which was as affectionately returned. It began to look as though the ball would be a very pleasant experience.

Then Echo came into the room, and they turned to admire her in her cloud of white silk mull, a necklace of pearls her only ornament. The child resembled a veritable fairy princess, and couldn't have been further removed from the danger of being thought an insipid debutante, though she was tied by convention to the demurest of gowns and the simplest of jewels.

Carrisbrooke met the ladies in the drawing room where they eventually gathered to await those guests who had been honoured with an invitation to dine before the ball. He complimented the appearance of each according to her situation: Echo was "bound to be a heartbreaker"; his sister would "have every man in the place fighting for her favours"; and Miss Dalrymple was "every inch the distinguished authoress, and a diamond of the first water besides."

"Not quite an authoress, as my book is not due out until the day after tomorrow," was Sophia's answer to this flattery, uttered in as dry and satirical a tone as she could manage in her excitement.

Carrisbrooke favoured her with his most caressing glance, bowed over her hand and solicited that same hand for the first dance of the evening. "For I know Echo won't want to open the ball with her old uncle, and Amarantha and I have a pact never to dance together, formed in our early youth and thus far never broken," he said, qualifying his invitation with a grin.

"I would certainly be conspicuous dancing with you," was Sophia's light response, as she tried to ignore the interested and suddenly sharp glances of Amarantha and even Echo, "and you know I've decided to be a sort of auditor at this party."

"Which your host refuses to allow," retorted Carrisbrooke.

"Any young lady you distinguish *will* stand out in the crowd, brother," said Amarantha. "But I agree with you that it's no more than proper to open the evening with your house guest. It is indeed, Sophia," she repeated with a very encouraging look at the young lady. "Come, now, you can't hope to be invisible."

"And Uncle has a *tendre* for you," piped up Echo in a disarmingly innocent way that caused the others to writhe—Sophia and Carrisbrooke in embarrassment, and Amarantha in chagrin, for it so happened that her ladyship was beginning to have definite matchmaking thoughts in the direction of Sophia and her brother and didn't like to see Echo kill such an intriguingly original possibility before it had time to take root.

Luckily, anything said by Echo could be treated as childish prattle, regardless of the fact that the chit had turned seventeen and was showing a most unusual shrewdness. Amarantha proceeded to do this, laughing and saying lightly, "What gentleman wouldn't form a *tendre* for our Miss Dalrymple, so charming as she looks tonight. Now, Sophia, why not dance? Charles won't bite you.''

"Ah, sister, be sure of nothing in this world," Carrisbrooke said wickedly, with a meaningful leer at Sophia, which was interpreted by his sister as facetious and by his intended partner as probably meaning great mischief. "The first dance, then, madam? I'll haul you out of any corner you think to hide in."

And Sophia had to give over with no further argument, for she heard the first guests beginning to arrive.

Some twenty people sat down with the marquis and his family for the intimate two-course dinner which was to precede the dancing, and when this was over Carrisbrooke and his womenfolk took their places on the landing to greet a fast-growing throng of elegant ladies, hatchet-faced dowagers, demure debutantes, supercilious dandies, elderly roués and all of the other notables who made up the London *beau monde*.

Lady Amarantha was flattered beyond anything when two of the royal dukes arrived betimes—for the royals usually made only a quick pass through any party; and Echo was thrown into alt when a dashing young Spanish count, attached to the embassy, solicited her hand for the first dance. Any fool could see that Almirez was the handsomest man in London, apart from her Uncle Charles, and he was reputed to be fabulously rich besides. Carrisbrooke was kept busy in fending off the jovial comments of his cronies, who frankly snickered to see him doing the pretty at a come-out ball.

Just when the crush was growing unbearable—the sure sign of a successful gathering—Sophia ventured from the alcove where she had demurely secreted her-

self after dinner and stepped hesitantly into the throng
of fashionables, feeling shy and more gauche than she
had in years, but determined to pass among these elegant strangers and gain the side of Lady Amarantha, who she supposed was her chaperon.

She noticed more than a few people staring at her as
she went by and thought with chagrin that they must
be doing so because she was so obviously alone. It was
a relief to gain the ballroom entrance just as Lady
Amarantha, accompanied by Echo, was descending
the stairs.

Her ladyship stretched out her hand. "Sophia, my
dear, you're just in time. If my girl's romantic and
distressingly handsome cavalier will but come to fetch
her, I'll give the signal for the first set. Ah, *señor
conde*!"

The young Spaniard approached and was presented to Miss Dalrymple. Sophia had to stifle a giggle as the gentleman, who couldn't be more than
twenty-one and had already cultivated a dangerously
suave manner, bowed and murmured an extravagant
compliment her way before tenderly taking charge of
Echo and leading the girl out to the floor.

Sophia stared after Almirez's tall, dark and very
erect form. He was really a very charming young man
despite the fact that he slightly overdid the manners
which matched his looks. His faultless evening dress,
augmented by the several foreign orders displayed on
his chest, showed his straight, slim figure to advantage.

"Quite a feather in my girl's cap," whispered
Amarantha with an indulgent smile at the young pair.
"That boy is as rich as Croesus, besides being the
youngest member of the embassy to have whatever

those intriguing orders on his chest are, and every matchmaking mama in the ton has already discovered that Spain would be the perfect home for her daughter.''

''And have *you*?''

''By no means, but it *is* gratifying to see all the dowagers in the room looking daggers at me. Ah, here comes Charles to take you to the floor.'' Lady Amarantha's eyes held a special twinkle as she announced her brother's approach.

Sophia saw this pointed look, and her heart sank. It would be so uncomfortable to have her hostess encourage a supposed flirtation between Carrisbrooke and herself. How it would make Sophia writhe, given the true circumstances! Well, one could be extra cold to the marquis, and that would kill Lady Amarantha's hopes. The gloved hand Sophia presently held out to Lord Carrisbrooke was deliberately languid, and her expression was chill indeed. The marquis's eyes held their usual teasing light, and Sophia guessed that he, at least, was not fooled. She knew that she was blushing even more than usual as she and her host took their places as second couple in the opening set.

Meanwhile, the voice of an urbane, unattached peer said to Lady Amarantha, ''Good Lord, who is that lovely creature dancing with Carrisbrooke? Will you introduce me?''

Lady Amarantha's eyes narrowed. ''My word, Humphries, I shouldn't think you'd want to bother,'' she said with a shrug. ''That is Miss Dalrymple, my neighbour in the country. Penniless daughter of the vicar and over one and twenty. She isn't hanging out for admirers in the least; she has merely come up for a short visit to see a little bit of Town life.''

Lord Humphries, who *was*, as everyone knew, hanging out for a wife, nodded brightly. "And you will present me?"

Amarantha sighed in vexation. It was not at all convenient to her as yet unhatched plans that Charles should have rivals. But by the time the set ended she could see that he was going to, for she was surrounded not only by her personal coterie of six or seven admirers, but by no less than ten gentlemen who had demanded, begged or coerced an introduction to Sophia Dalrymple.

That lady, quite unaware that she was the object of any but offhand attention—for nobody who danced with Carrisbrooke could go unnoticed—had been enjoying wholeheartedly her first dance in a long while. Carrisbrooke was an attentive and impeccably correct partner, addressing only polite commonplaces to her when they met in the movements of the dance. His gloved hand did seem to burn hers on those occasions when they did have to touch, but that was no fault of his. She was mightily relieved by the marquis's calm manners, having assumed that he would use this occasion to badger her with thinly veiled allusions to their proposed "nearer connection," and she felt guilty for not trusting that he would act the gentleman. It was with a light heart that she accepted Carrisbrooke's arm back to the side of Lady Amarantha, who was, she observed fondly, surrounded by a positive phalanx of masculine admirers.

Lady Amarantha beckoned her brother and his partner with a resigned smile. "I warn you, Charles, bespeak a second dance with Miss Dalrymple now if you desire one, for I'm about to present her to at least ten gentlemen who are clamouring to meet her."

Carrisbrooke grinned at the astonished Sophia.
"Delighted. The first waltz, then, Miss Dalrymple,
and supper?" And with a cheerful nod to the assem-
bled group he walked off to a knot of toplofty dowagers and dutifully began to make his charm felt.

Sophia had no time to watch him or to see where she
went, as she had planned to do: she was too busy
curtseying and murmuring polite nothings to the
gentlemen, most of them titled, personable and over
thirty, though there were one or two gaping youths
who would have done better to worship at the shrine
of little Echo. The countrified Miss Dalrymple had
never met so many men at once in her life, and she
couldn't begin to remember all their names. She was
pleased, confused and startled by the extravagant
compliments paid her by all and sundry, especially
when one frank boy made a remark which indicated
that her status as a penniless spinster was not unknown to the gentlemen.

As Lord Humphries, claiming the privilege of first
in line, prepared to lead Sophia off to the quadrille,
Lady Amarantha grasped her sleeve and whispered in
her ear, "Did I forget to tell you, my love, that next to
Echo you're the most glorious creature in the room
tonight? So stupid of us to think no one would notice."

Sophia danced, chatted and laughed with one man
after another. It was extraordinary what a success she
was having! At the rural assemblies she had attended
in the past, where most of the men in the room were
family friends and well aware of the state of her father's finances, she had never enjoyed more than what
she had considered her fair share of popularity. Thus
she had never developed an elevated idea of her own

attractions, and that these many men, ranging in type from middle-aged dandies to fresh-faced ensigns, should consider her worthy of more than a passing glance was amazing. In fact, it was even amusing.

Sophia's brow furrowed momentarily as she worked in her mind to discover the reason for all this attention. She *was* wearing the most becoming and modish gown she had ever owned—that must count for something. And nobody here had seen her before, and novelty did have its appeal. She was also of a greater age and at least nominally more sophisticated than the many young girls in their first seasons who dotted the room in pink and white muslins. And added to all this, men were notorious followers. A young woman distinguished by the marquis of Carrisbrooke would no doubt be sought after if she were a bracket-faced creature in a torn gown.

Thus ran Sophia's thoughts, and her partner of the moment called her dreamy-eyed expression mysterious and alluring. She spoiled this effect quite dramatically by laughing in the gentleman's face, and he was so enchanted that he demanded a second dance.

Soon the first waltz struck up, and Carrisbrooke moved across the crowded floor to claim Miss Dalrymple. "At last," he murmured as he took her hand and clasped her much closer than the prescribed twelve inches. They moved away in time to the music.

Sophia's only answer was a somewhat nervous smile.

Encouraged by this, the marquis went on, "Of course, this can't be as interesting as the first time I clasped you in my arms. But I'm comforted by the knowledge that it won't be the last." He smiled enigmatically.

"Sir, this isn't the time—" Sophia began in an undertone as she followed his lead round the floor.

"Ah, but it's always the time," retorted Carrisbrooke with a deliberately lascivious chuckle. "Permit me to be at least the twentieth man tonight to assure you, my love, that you're the most enchanting young woman to grace a London ballroom in years. Or possibly ever."

"Thank you, sir, I'll take that in the joking spirit in which it was meant," said Sophia primly, casting down her eyes.

She got through the waltz with nothing worse than those few remarks from the marquis, and he delivered her to her next partner. But not an hour later her mischievous host captured Sophia once again. As she returned into the ballroom from the ladies' retiring room, she was summarily snatched into a dimly lit antechamber by a familiar, strong pair of arms.

"My dear," groaned Carrisbrooke, crushing his quarry to his chest, partially to hide from her the laughter in his eyes, "one kiss and I'll let you go. You must grant me that, for you've inflamed my passions with your beauty, you know."

But Sophia had pulled back in his arms in time to see the deviltry shining from his brown eyes, and accordingly shook her head and gave a light laugh. "Then you wouldn't wish to inflame them further, my lord," she said matter-of-factly, pushing her hands against his chest and trying to ignore the rapid beating of her suddenly unmanageable heart.

Carrisbrooke paid no attention to her words. He held her more closely than ever, and turned her face up to his with a gentle hand. Then he kissed her slowly, deliberately, in a style which he knew would earn him a box on the ear from any other lady.

But his Sophia couldn't stop her warm response, the marquis noted with delight when he loosened his hold after several very interesting minutes. "One day we'll do much more than kiss," he murmured in a voice which he took care to make throb with passion. He then politely caught Miss Dalrymple in his arms again, for her knees had apparently buckled.

"Sir, you simply must stop tormenting me like this," sighed Sophia, looking away in confusion. Good heavens! If the rest of lovemaking was anything like this, she had certainly got more than she bargained for on that long-ago summer day when she had promised to sell the marquis her virtue. Why, oh why, had she done it? Then she remembered her book, due to appear in a few days. The first of many books, she fondly hoped, and the beginning of a new life in which she would have to answer to no one. And all due to the bargain she had struck with this infuriating man.

"It's quite a good sign that I torment you, you know," stated Carrisbrooke blandly. With a connoisseur's eye he made some small adjustment to Sophia's dress, disarranged by the embrace, and tucked a curl back into her headdress. "Gives one every reason to expect our liaison will be a pleasant one."

With a tortured "Oh!" Sophia turned on her heel and ran back to the ballroom, where a dozen men who had seen her come out of the antechamber into which Carrisbrooke had previously disappeared, and who now thought the worst, all clamoured for her favours.

The evening was "a triumph," a complacent Lady Amarantha announced to her daughter and Miss Dalrymple when the three ladies were at long last sitting in a quiet corner of the otherwise deserted drawing room in the small hours of the morning, Carrisbrooke having followed a group of his brother officers to Watier's. "Echo is well on her way to becoming the belle of the season," said Amarantha with justifiable pride. Echo, stolidly munching her way through a final plate of lobster patties, looked up with a smile. "And as for Sophia! My dear, you might want to revise your position on marriage. More than one gentleman seemed quite taken with your charms. We ought to have foreseen it."

"I shall never marry," said Sophia quietly. Echo stared, and Lady Amarantha looked wise and nodded. The two different reactions to her words might have caused Sophia embarrassment if she hadn't been too tired to notice. She stifled a yawn.

"That's as may be," Lady Amarantha said, her voice casual. "Oh, by the bye, my dear, did Lord Bell manage to speak to you? A cousin of yours, I believe. He paid his devoirs to me most prettily, and mentioned he wasn't able to get close to you because of the 'multitudes of your adorers.' His very words."

"Why, no, I didn't see the gentleman. Not that I'd know him, for we've never met," replied Sophia with a marked lack of interest. She had no desire to meet the odious creature who had refused—through his secretary—to patronize the work of his young relation. She was glad she had missed him at the ball.

CHAPTER NINE

SOPHIA MIGHT NOT have been been anxious to make the acquaintance of her distant relation Lord Bell, but that worthy baron had other ideas. On the very day after Echo Burroughs's come-out ball the gentleman was requesting admittance to Carrisbrooke House.

The butler, mortally tired of opening the door to positive floods of callers, bearers of flowers and deliverers of *billets doux*, was nevertheless well trained enough to betray no sign of boredom as he showed the latest male visitor into the drawing room, where the ladies were receiving and at present sat with seven or eight other gentlemen and two formidable dowagers.

Lord Bell paused on the threshhold. He was a man of some forty summers who had graced society for years, and his stately figure, with its slight tendency to *embonpoint*, his light hair flawlessly arranged *au coup de vent* and the exquisite cut of his clothes, were so well-known in the drawing rooms of the ton as to make this conscious moment of display virtually unnecessary. But the personality of the baron was not such that he could resist even so fleeting a moment as the centre of attention.

Breaking his pose in the doorway, he hastened in a flurry of polite chivalry to the chair of Lady Amarantha Burroughs and made a killing bow. His squarish face and shrewd blue eyes were carefully suggestive of warm regard. Next he bowed deeper still before her ladyship's charming daughter, giving the child her due as the new Incomparable of the season. The girl's nymphlike form was surrounded by an honour guard of three junior officers, as well as Count Almirez and a chubby young dandy who was offering the young lady a piece of marchpane from the box he obviously kept by him at all times. After greeting the two Burroughs ladies, Bell sought out his distant connection, Miss Dalrymple.

He had been much struck by the lady's ravishing appearance the night before in that revealing and stylish ball gown; he was somewhat surprised to find her charms not at all diminished by the less modish morning gown in which she was draped today. "My dear cousin," the baron said in a remarkably deep, somewhat theatrical voice, "how do you do? Desolated to have missed a dance with you last night, but I hope to have the honour sometime soon. May I sit beside you? How are your dear parents?"

Sophia, noting with amusement how quickly the place next to her was vacated by the very young gentleman who had been regaling her with tales of his Oxford days—which she suspected were not quite over—was pleased to inform Lord Bell that her father was well, but desolated to have to remind him that her mother, whose kin he was, had died five years ago.

Lord Bell cleared his throat loudly, said insincerely, "Ah, yes, so sad," and then turned the subject. "Well, my dear, I am delighted to make your acquaintance at last. What do you say to furthering our cousinly relationship by a drive in the Park this afternoon?"

Sophia paused to consider. She had no wish to be distinguished by this baron, whose manner she didn't like. He seemed to be much too oily, and his reputation wasn't of the most spotless, according to her father. Of course, Mr. Dalrymple's idea of a major transgression was probably a tendency to gamble or travel on Sunday, so that the Reverend Mr. Dalrymple's opinion wasn't a large consideration. On the other side of the coin, Lord Bell was a personable man, and a relation. Too, Echo and Amarantha had been regaling Sophia with tales of Hyde Park, and how amusing it was to drive there at the fashionable hour.

"I'd enjoy that," she said on impulse, a small part of her relishing the fact that Lord Carrisbrooke just might hear of her outing and be displeased, or at least surprised, that she had caught the eye of her noble cousin.

"Splendid. Shall we say five?" Lord Bell smiled and inclined his head in approval, and had soon moved across the room to greet an acquaintance. The young man whose place he had usurped dived back to it forthwith, for the callow gentleman was finding Miss Dalrymple to be a rare good-natured sort of person, though an "older woman," and she was so attentive to his tales that he really couldn't help spending all his time at her side.

"Driving with Lord Bell? Well, you aren't seven years old, my dear, and I suppose you know what you're doing," was Lady Amarantha's comment when Sophia later told her of the afternoon's plan. "Wear your best bonnet, and take care to remind the man he's your kin."

Sophia dimpled. "I gather the baron isn't altogether harmless?"

Amarantha shrugged and replied, "Well, there are stories. But once I put it about that you're his cousin, no one will think the worse of you for driving with him. It will be good for you to see the Park, and I don't find it amiss to have you there today. I'm not going, and Echo will be driving with Almirez. You can keep an eye out for her."

"I'll certainly give her my most severe and duenna-ish look when we meet," said Sophia with a laugh. She then disappeared into her room to put together something to wear.

When, at a bit after five, she started down the stairs to meet Bell, Sophia wasn't satisfied with her appearance, but she consoled herself with the thought that she hadn't come to Town to cut a dash, but merely to observe society, gather material for future novels and play an unobtrusive role at a few social events. Her sage-green bonnet, purchased since her arrival in London with the carefully hoarded remains of her dress allowance, *was* all the crack with its blush-pink ruched lining and matching satin ribbons. But the white cambric gown she wore with it was decidedly lacking in town bronze, as was the dark green pelisse that topped the dress. However, the colour scheme was not unpleasant, and her kid gloves and newish half-boots were beyond reproach.

She knew that her cousin was a recognized dandy, and *he* didn't act displeased to be seen with her, which relieved her uneasy mind. Bell greeted her with a flourish and handed her out of the house and into a smart curricle drawn by an unexceptionable pair of greys. Sophia was a bit concerned when his lordship told the tiger to await their return at Carrisbrooke House, but reasoned that a man who had met her but that morning couldn't be thinking to indulge in the sort of familiarities that such behaviour normally must denote. And he *was* a relation.

The ride from Grosvenor Square to Hyde Park was short, and Lord Bell's curricle was soon passing through the gate of that most fashionable of promenades. Sophia looked about with avid interest at the crowded scene before her. Surely everyone with the slightest pretension to fashion must be here today. Curricles, phaetons, landaus and tilburies jammed the road, each more showy than the last; the bridle trails were alive with male and female equestrians, all fashionable, all on highly bred cattle that deserved better than the snail-like pace forced on them by the crowded conditions; and the tree-lined alleys and expanses of grassy lawn were dotted with carefully dressed pedestrians. Sophia had to laugh to herself as the thought struck her that everyone in this slowly milling crowd was no doubt engaged in their only "exercise" of the day.

Apart from such irreverent thoughts, she found the sight of so many brilliant people as confusing and exciting as it had been the previous night at the ball. In an effort at proper social behaviour she began to try to distinguish one face from another and recognized several people from the night before, who returned her friendly nods with varying degrees of hauteur.

"There is little Miss Burroughs and her Spanish cavalier," Lord Bell leaned over to say, and Sophia's eyes turned in the direction of his pointing hand. Yes, there was Echo, looking very pleased with herself. The child had on an extremely modish carriage dress cut *à la Hussar*, in a heavenly shade of blue that perfectly matched her eyes. Behind her on the extremely ornate and highly perched phaeton of black and silver perched her mother's footman, and close beside her sat the young Count Almirez, as exotically dashing and, well, pantherlike as he had been the night before. He looked as frankly pleased as Echo.

The count's vehicle was approaching Lord Bell's, and the two gentlemen reined in for a moment to allow their ladies to speak.

"Oh, Sophia," enthused Echo, leaning across her escort's lap, "having admirers is extremely amusing. I'm so glad I'm old enough."

Sophia burst out laughing before she could stop herself.

The young Spaniard flashed his fair companion a tender look and bowed to the older lady. "Ah, Miss, er, Dalrymple. The *señorita* honours me with her approbation. And it is true I must style myself her admirer. Her slave."

"There! Isn't that the funniest thing?" cried Echo with a giggle. "Now do let's go on, sir, for I know Mama will want to feed us when you take me home."

Sophia waved away the artless pair with much amusement, and she and Lord Bell shared a very adult laugh. "An engaging little creature, your friend," the baron said indulgently. "Already breaking hearts, if I don't miss my guess, and the observations I make are seldom wrong, Cousin Sophia."

Starting at this unlicensed use of her Christian name, Sophia chose to ignore the familiarity and answered, "Echo is certainly bound to have a great success. And she'll enjoy it so much! The child was quite bored in the schoolroom—for I've known her for

years—and it seems she must have been waiting all
that time to put her true talents to work among the
ton.''

''And she will certainly be its greatest ornament,''
proclaimed Lord Bell with practised gallantry. He then
gave Sophia a bold, appraising glance. ''And you,
Cousin? What motives bring you to Town?''

Sophia shrugged in an offhand manner. ''Why, the
usual,'' she said in surprise. ''Visiting my friends,
seeing the sights.''

His lordship nodded. ''Not, by any chance, publishing your novel?''

''My dear sir! To think you'd remember that,'' Sophia exclaimed, not at all pleased. Her book was to
appear on the morrow, but she saw no reason to tell
this man her secret; not after he had so negligently refused to help her in the project. She still seethed at the
memory of his secretary's cold letter to her father.

Lord Bell smiled in an intimate fashion that disturbed his companion further. ''Why, how should I
not remember? I only regret my hasty decision not to
involve myself in your scheme. Had I known what a
lovely and obviously intelligent creature my unknown
cousin was, I should never have refused. I do beg your
pardon.''

Sophia said nothing.

Encouraged by this silence, Bell went on, ''Naturally, now that I've met you, I wouldn't be at all averse
to putting a word or two in Murray's ear, or Eger-
ton's. I am sure that you would be properly, er, grateful for such little attentions on my part, and as you are
my cousin, it would cause no undue comment if we
two were to be seen often in each other's company—
or indeed were observed leaving the wrong sort of

place together." He leered, and with no further ado, grasped Sophia's hand with the one of his that wasn't holding the ribbons.

"Sir!" gasped Sophia, withdrawing her hand with a violent tug. "Good heavens! Remember that you're speaking to a relation, and a vicar's daughter. You simply can't be suggesting what I think you are."

Lord Bell smiled enigmatically, and Sophia was suddenly very aware of the lines of dissipation etched into his personable face.

She was also sensible of ever so slight a feeling of guilt at her own hypocrisy. If she weren't mistaken, and she didn't think she was, Lord Bell had just made a most improper and insulting overture to her, and she had repelled it with all the fitting moral outrage she possessed. But she was uncomfortably aware that she was engaged to perform with Lord Carrisbrooke in the same improper way that her leering cousin had just been so bold as to put forth, and this one at her own instigation!

Bell was speaking again, his voice low and caressing. He leaned toward Sophia, seeming not to notice how quickly she edged away. "My dear, we are not very closely related, and I know you're totally without fortune and much past the age which you can expect to be married for your beauty alone. You must lead a lonely life. It might not be so unpleasant, you know, to do me one or two favours in exchange for becoming a famous authoress."

"I have no wish for fame, sir," said Sophia tightly.

"Money, then. And might it not be amusing to go about on my arm?"

It must be admitted that Lord Bell was beginning to allow himself a few fanciful dreams about setting up this beautiful relation of his as the most dashing barque of frailty on the Town; and he would be the only one in his set whose mistress was an authoress besides being a regular *nonpareil*. Yes, she would be ruined and cast off from her family and friends, but such inconveniences to her meant little to Lord Bell, who pragmatically judged that the compensatory value of the position of Fashionable Impure, plus of course his own suave attentions, would be worth a few sacrifices to one whose only other fate was to live out her days as a country spinster.

He had been concocting this idea of Miss Dalrymple's future ever since he had seen her the night before, happened to recall her name and a certain diffident letter he had received from her father, then concluded that her literary ambitions would be the best instrument to his hand in any plan to rob her of her virtue. And she wouldn't be getting a bad bargain, he reminded himself as what little was left of his conscience baulked at the idea of leading a respectable spinster down the garden path. He had never failed to do the right thing by his convenients, and his association with her would bring her to the attention of many possible protectors.

Sophia was in the grip of a very annoying attack of self-disgust—for it was shameful to realize that her suggestions to Carrisbrooke had been no more innocent than Lord Bell's to her—and she considered in stony silence what sort of thing she might say to depress her cousin's pretensions. She couldn't let him know that she had already got the patronage she craved; he would be bound to ask awkward questions, and she didn't want him to put it about that her novel had just appeared—as it would tomorrow, she reminded herself in momentary elation. She had always had a strong desire for anonymity, but it was greater than ever now that she was out in society, in however small a way. She hated to think of being annoyed by the patronizing comments of those who would be incredulous or amused that a country nobody's scribblings had made it into print; and she had long planned on the secret happiness she would derive from listening to the honest critiques of people who might pick up her book and judge it purely by its merit. She decided, therefore, to placate Lord Bell with an outright lie.

"I've put aside my little literary endeavours," she said with a demure look. "I'm afraid there wasn't much to it after all. So I can't ask you to patronize what doesn't exist any longer. I . . . I burned my little novel."

"Oh." Lord Bell frowned in thought. This sensible refusal was not at all what he had expected from the lady. He had thought to hear one of two things only: either a scathing lecture expressive of all sorts of puritan virtues and outraged morality, possibly including a slap on the face and a refusal ever to countenance his presence again; or a blushing and shy acceptance of his *carte blanche*.

Sophia, for her part, was too honest to act the injured maiden. The knowledge that she had already engineered her own ruin in quite a cold-blooded and calculating way made her unable to react with the proper horror to proposals which would have thrown any lady of strict principles into the vapours. Her only anxiety was to prevent the renewal of these lewd suggestions and to escape from the curricle as soon as possible.

"Yes, I burned it," she sighed in answer to her companion's surprise, "and naturally I have no reason now to wish your patronage. But I do thank you for the thought, and I promise, my lord, to forget what you said." She smiled in an ingenuous fashion, noticing in relief that Lord Bell was heading his cattle for the nearest gate.

"Of course, my dear," said Bell smoothly, flashing his cousin a confused glance. She had set him down, in a way; but she hadn't been overly cross with him. This could only mean that his proposals hadn't been altogether unwelcome. It was a shame that she couldn't accept them under the guise of helping along her little literary pretensions, but it appeared she might still be brought to heel, and such a lovely and untouched mistress would be worth the waiting for.

Bell came to a practical decision. He would follow this young woman's lead and act toward her with every appearance of cousinly mildness, until an expedient moment came to renew his offer.

CHAPTER TEN

THE NEXT MORNING Sophia, well recovered from her drive in the Park with her boldly lecherous kinsman, sat down with the Burroughs ladies to a late breakfast. Lady Amarantha was sifting through a mountain of invitations and paying scant attention to her plate; Echo, plying her fork in her usual industrious manner, was staring off into space; and Miss Dalrymple, who had never been more nervous in her life, was shakily drinking coffee, and halfway thinking she ought to call for a mug of ale. Nothing could turn her mind from the fact that today was the day her novel was scheduled to make its appearance, and she could hardly contain her impatience and her sense of pleasurable dread. Lord Carrisbrooke had gone out to Murray's to get the ladies their copy, and Sophia had never been so anxious to see the gentleman in her life.

All thoughts of her afternoon ride with Lord Bell had flown right out of her mind.

"We'd have to be at least three more people to respond to all these invitations," Lady Amarantha said with a satisfied sigh, laying down a card unmistakably embossed with a ducal crest. "Echo, you're well on your way to becoming the debutante of the season. Oh, do stop eating."

"But, Mama, this is breakfast," returned Echo in surprise, pouring herself a third cup of chocolate as she dexterously reached for the ham platter with the other hand. "It is exciting to be admired. Do you know that Almirez sent me two dozen white roses, Mama? With some sort of note about my purity and innocence. And there are lots more bouquets out in the hall."

Lady Amarantha smiled. "I've already looked through them, child, and two are actually for your mama! Not to mention the red roses Lord Bell sent Sophia."

"He did?" Sophia choked. She had been too nervous this morning to look through the flowers other than to note that there were quite as many as yesterday morning. "Was there a note?"

"No, merely his card. I hope the man hasn't tried to take liberties with you?" Amarantha's eyes were suddenly sharp with concern.

"By no means," lied Sophia, her brow furrowing slightly. Why on earth, knowing that she would never countenance coming under his protection, would Lord Bell be sending her flowers? She prayed that it was merely a peacemaking gesture and not a sign that his hopes of seducing her hadn't been effectively dashed by her quelling manners of the day before.

"Good. Now tell me, what are we to do about this wealth of invitations? They all include you, Sophia, too, and I know you came to Town determined not to go into society. What am I to say to people? Do change your mind," said Lady Amarantha in her most persuasive tone.

Sophia shook her head and smiled. "I simply can't, my lady. I don't have the means, as you know. And I won't be staying very much longer."

"You can wear my clothes," put in Echo helpfully, as usual getting to the crux of the argument in a disarmingly direct fashion.

Laughing, Sophia responded, "Not unless I suddenly shrink by half a head. And it isn't only the clothes, dear, it's that I live a very retired sort of life, not in the least in the style of yours and your mama's, and it wouldn't be, well, seemly for me to go jauntering about as though I were a young girl come to Town for the season."

"But that's exactly what you are, in a way," protested Lady Amarantha, Echo merely nodding seriously and applying herself to another slice of toast. "At least that is the way in which all our friends seem determined to see you after your raging success at Echo's ball."

"Raging success! Oh, no," said Sophia. "A few gentlemen simply distinguished me because I'd danced with your brother, and we know he could bring anyone into fashion."

"Well, that my brother is definitely top of the trees, as they say, is not to be disputed," admitted Amarantha with a frank nod. She stole a glance of maddening slyness at Sophia and wondered if the dear creature realized how obvious her own *tendre* for Charles was—at least to a seasoned observer of romance such as herself.

Amarantha, daughter of the proud and noble house of Carrisbrooke, was not exhibiting the normal alarm one might expect any highborn lady to feel at the knowledge which had come to her recently: that her untrappable brother had been captivated by a penniless miss from an undistinguished family, and that the miss in question was head over heels in love with him.

Amarantha did not know if the participants in this drama were as yet aware of their sentiments, but she thought not. This made their little love story all the more amusing.

The suspicion that Sophia loved Carrisbrooke had been growing in Amarantha ever since she had read the girl's novel, a piece of artistry that struck her as wish-fulfilment at its most blatant, and made her long to know when Sophia might have met—or seen—Charles and found the material upon which to base her "earl" of the novel. The poor but gently bred heroine of *The River Garden* eventually captured her nobleman—or was captured by him, it wasn't too clear—due to a series of skilful machinations by the book's minor characters, finely drawn comic figures who seemed as real as the people Amarantha met every day. But Lady Amarantha had no idea how such an easy happy ending was to come about for the real-life nobleman and impecunious young woman; she only knew that she would help it along as best she could. She had many reasons for doing so, including her liking for Sophia, her astonished observation of real interest—at last!—in Carrisbrooke's attitude toward a decent woman and her irrepressible, somewhat mischievous desire for a scandalous marriage such as this would be to enliven her season and make the cats stare. The marquis of Carrisbrooke might marry where he wished, after all. The family had no need to buy either fortune or social status.

Had Sophia had even an inkling that the marquis's sister considered her a fit bride for his lordship, she would have been ready to sink, given her own knowledge of the terms upon which she stood with the gentleman. She had seen Amarantha's speculative looks and cringed at them, but she supposed they only denoted curiosity, and that her ladyship expected some amusement from seeing her brother flirt with their spinster guest. Sophia couldn't even begin to imagine what Lady Amarantha would say if she knew that she was sitting at table with her brother's future mistress.

But of course poor innocent Amarantha had no idea of this, Sophia thought with a fond look at the carefree way the lady was pawing through that stack of cards, all unaware that she was harbouring a light woman under her—or, that is, her brother's—roof.

Amarantha looked up again to continue her argument. "But however you got brought into fashion, Sophia, there you are. You must force yourself to respond to at least some of the requests for your company. My wardrobe is at your disposal, for you and *I* are of a height, and I am going to insist."

Sophia had to smile and weaken; she didn't want to be ungracious and rude. "I suppose I might accept perhaps one or two more engagements in the time I'm here."

"One or two more a day, I assume you mean."

The ladies disputed good-humouredly for several minutes more, and Sophia finally agreed to attend those social events which Lady Amarantha, in her superior knowledge of the ton, should consider most important. But as her wardrobe wouldn't allow her to live a complete whirl and she must refuse to go about all the time dressed in her hostess's clothes, she was resolved to limit herself rather stringently. They were just concluding the details of their agreement when Carrisbrooke strode into the room, clasping in one hand three slim volumes bound in brown calf.

The marquis, his face alight with pleasure, walked straight to Sophia's chair and set the books before her. "*The River Garden*, by a lady," he said in the same tone of voice in which his butler might have announced royalty.

Sophia looked up at him, her eyes full of happiness and a tear trembling on her lashes. Restraining himself with difficulty from seizing her in his arms then and there, the marquis took refuge in humour, grinning and giving her a wink before he moved to his place at the head of the table and poured himself a cup of coffee.

"Well, my dear, do let us see," said Lady Amarantha excitedly, reaching down the table, and she was soon leafing through volume 2 with her paper-knife, while Echo examined the cover of volume 3 with polite interest.

As for Sophia, she sat quite still with volume 1 in her hands, holding the book as if it were a baby bird. Finally she was able to look at the marquis and give him her most dazzling smile. "My dear sir, thank you," she said.

Carrisbrooke inclined his head, returning her smile. "It is I who thank you," he answered with a secret hint of mischief lurking in his eyes.

Sophia looked down at the table and fumbled in her reticule for a paper-cutter.

When at length the group rose from the table, Amarantha declared herself to be bursting with curiosity as to what people would say if they knew that the quiet Miss Dalrymple was an authoress; and this reminded the quiet Miss Dalrymple to extract her ladyship's promise—and the marquis's—that they would carry her secret to the grave. Echo had already left the room, or she would have been formally sworn to silence also.

"Wait a few days, and then let's start asking people if they've picked up anything new at Hatchard's, or at Hookham's," suggested Carrisbrooke. "This patronage of the arts does have its interest, as does the cloak-and-dagger business of keeping it a secret. I'm no novel reader—"

"Yes, Charles, we both know that," interrupted Amarantha.

"—but I can see that I'm going to be quizzing those of my friends who are about their reading habits. It's quite exciting, Miss Dalrymple."

"It certainly is," the fledgling authoress had to agree.

"Beyond a doubt," put in Amarantha. She hooked her arm through Sophia's and began to head out of the breakfast room, saying that they would go to her boudoir now to look through clothes. "I suppose we'll see you this evening, Charles?" she said over her shoulder.

"As a matter of fact, I must beg for a little of Miss Dalrymple's time right now," Carrisbrooke contested. "Murray has one or two things he wants me to pass on to the author, information about one thing and another. I have it all written down in my study, if you would follow me there, madam?" He bowed to Sophia.

"Yes, do go on. I daresay it won't take long," Lady Amarantha added. "I'll have Ross take out the things I mean for you to have, dear, and you may join us whenever you're ready."

Sophia nodded obediently and went off after the marquis in the direction of his study. She was still clutching the precious volume 1 in her hands as a sort of charm against ... against what? She wondered if Carrisbrooke meant to seduce her at once in the study. Oddly enough, this prospect didn't distress her as much as she considered it ought to.

Moments later, Carrisbrooke closed the door of his private room with a snap, leaned against it and surveyed the lady who stood facing him. "Well, Miss Dalrymple," he said with an odd light in his dark eyes, "we come to the question of our bargain."

Sophia surveyed his tall figure. "Yes," she said in a voice which, to her horror, squeaked a little.

The marquis chuckled, and he ran his eyes over her in his usual thorough manner, seeming to find no fault with her simple morning costume or what was under it. "I'm glad you're pleased with your book, my dear. But I think I have the best of this agreement," he said as he stepped forward.

Sophia was not at all surprised to find herself being roughly clasped in his arms. It was a wonder to her that he had even bothered to lead up to this action at all, considering his behaviour the other night in the antechamber of the ballroom, not to mention his many other thinly veiled hints of the rapidly approaching time for their bargain to be kept. Well, she was ready.

With no more than a passing thought for her honour, now lost forever, Sophia lifted her face to receive Carrisbrooke's kiss, responding with a force which surprised him, to judge from his groan of pleasure as he murmured "My dear!" against her lips. But as he kissed her again and again, she felt something else stealing into her physical reaction to his caresses. Stunned, Sophia realized all of a sudden that what she was trying to express was not only passion, but affection. She pulled away in a sort of terror.

"You're perfectly right, my love," said Carrisbrooke, saluting her forehead gently. "This isn't the time or the place for our discreet arrangement to begin—though you're making it difficult for me to remember that." He laughed and took her face between his hands. "What," he said, seeing her worried expression, "backing out at this late date? I thought you were a woman of honour."

"Of course I am," exclaimed Sophia in confusion. "I'm not backing out. I'm merely nervous. Anyone might come in."

"That's true," agreed the marquis tamely. "And it isn't to be expected that you give yourself up to my savage desires on the study floor, or even the study sofa. I'm going to leave Town shortly to arrange a secluded country retreat which will be a more fitting setting for our *amours*."

Sophia was suddenly suspicious at the hint of humour in his words. "Are you altogether sure you haven't forgotten your end of this bargain, my lord?" she demanded. "You did promise not to ruin me publicly."

"Whatever gives you the idea that I would make this public?" queried the marquis with studied hauteur. He crossed to a nearby mirror and busied himself with the rearrangement of his neckcloth. "Spoiled a perfectly good Mathematical, Sophia, my dear," he said over his shoulder. "I'll have to change it to a *Trône d'Amour*."

Sophia gave a noisy sigh of vexation. "Might I go now?" she asked in a dangerously calm voice. "You didn't really have any message from Mr. Murray, did you?''

''Caught me out, my love. That was merely an excuse. Yes, you may go, after you come over here and give me one last kiss.'' Carrisbrooke turned from the mirror and smiled wickedly. Sophia stepped toward him, luckily unaware of how timid and skittish she appeared to the marquis's amused eye. He took her in his arms for a kiss that was fairly gentle for a change, and predominately tender.

As it happened, Sophia would rather not have been treated so preciously at this particular moment, for the gentleman's care of her was much more disturbing than the ruthless ardour he was wont to display. She walked out of the study in a daze, without a backward glance, and made for Lady Amarantha's dressing room.

Her cheeks were flaming, and her mind was spinning, for she didn't know how she would be able to go through with her end of the bargain. How could she give herself with businesslike detachment to a man she had just discovered she loved?

CHAPTER ELEVEN

LUCKILY FOR Sophia's peace of mind, she and Lord Carrisbrooke didn't cross paths again that day. His dinner and evening engagements led him in a different direction from the ladies, who were to attend a *musicale* at Lady Sefton's. This entertainment was the perfect sort for Sophia in her perturbed and excited state. First she milled about the Seftons' saloons for an hour with what seemed half of London. And when she found herself seated between Echo and Lady Amarantha listening to the indifferent performance of a Mozart *rondo* by an indifferent string quartet, she felt very fortunate to be where she was. Only an evening at home could have been more conducive to the sort of dreaming and contemplation which was all she was fit for, and which she was able to indulge in to the fullest in the Seftons' crowded salon.

The thrill of her book's appearance in printed form, an event she would have sworn could not be surpassed by anything, had been dwarfed for the moment in Sophia's mind by another momentous occurrence: the discovery that she loved the marquis. Anyone who had been privy to Sophia's conduct in the matter of Carrisbrooke might have come to such a conclusion much before this; however, Sophia, though astute enough in most of her dealings, hadn't considered such an explanation of her actions.

She had been aware of a certain physical attraction
to Carrisbrooke from the moment he had awakened
her so rudely in her father's garden, and she had admittedly indulged in fancies about him since her teens.
But her feelings for him, which she knew in her heart
had led her to offer her virginity to him and no other,
had been no more than the lust her father was wont to
preach against of a Sunday. Or so she had supposed.
The secret pleasure she took in Lord Carrisbrooke's
teasing, the rare serious conversations they had had
and the rapport they had seemed to find, the warm
feeling that always washed over her when he was in the
room, she had not stopped to interpret. But their
kisses in the study that morning had put an end to her
peace of mind. What she had intended as a passion-
ate prelude to their prearranged liaison, which she'd
still harboured hope would not take place, had ended
as her first conscious expression of love.

As the musicians initiated an uninspired *allegro*,
Sophia's cheeks reddened in memory of her behaviour in Carrisbrooke's study. She really knew very little of the physical side of love. Had the marquis been
able to read her emotions in her kiss? If so, how
dreadfully exposed she felt! She also sensed a nagging
disappointment in her lover-to-be. Wouldn't a man
worthy of one's love be too honourable to pirate the
respectability of an innocent lady of quality, no matter what bargain he had struck with said lady? Sternly
Sophia reminded herself that she had repeatedly assured the marquis that she was not going to back out
of their arrangement. If she had backed out—if she
were to do so even now—he would certainly act the

gentleman and forgive her. But was she going to back out? Her cheeks got even redder.

Through the maze of her thoughts Sophia heard her name being called. Blinking, she raised her eyes and noticed that the music had ended and that the audience was beginning the migration to the supper room. Echo had risen and was urging Miss Dalrymple and her mama to hurry along. "Almirez has promised to forage for all of us," the young lady said grandly, indicating with a negligent wave of her hand the handsome young diplomat, who had appeared behind her.

"That would never do, dear, for he'll hardly be able to lift *your* plate," said Lady Amarantha, laughing. "You children run ahead, and do procure Sophia and me places by you. Meanwhile I'll see if I can't snag us a pair of cavaliers." And Amarantha, who was feeling quite the thing that evening in an apricot-coloured satin cut very low, cast a speculative eye around the room and smiled at Sophia. "Dreaming, my dear?" she asked slyly.

"Oh! Yes, a little. The excitement of this morning, you know," said Sophia, aghast that her preoccupation was so evident.

"My dear cousin! And Lady Amarantha. Both of you as radiant as goddesses," a deep, dramatic voice exclaimed. Sophia, whirling around in surprise, saw Lord Bell smiling down at her in a most predatory way.

This was an odd turn of events; her kinsman's manner wasn't that of the lover scorned. He must still aspire to her favours. To stamp out any such wrong thinking on Lord Bell's part, Sophia made her greeting to him as cold as civility would allow. She was gratified when Lady Amarantha, following her lead, made her own devoirs in a glacial manner.

However, Lord Bell was undeterred by what he chose to believe was only a becoming modesty in his cousin: a very proper, if somewhat starchy, unwillingness to flirt with him in public. Lady Amarantha's frosty manner didn't deter him in the least, it being her usual. He smiled even more broadly as he offered the ladies his company at supper.

"We can hardly say no," contested Lady Amarantha with a sigh, "but do be so good, sir, as to round up one of your friends to partner Sophia. We aren't of a mind to share you."

Sophia gave a silent thanks to her ladyship for taking on herself the escort of the dangerous Lord Bell, and she became even more resigned to her wolfish cousin's company when a young man of her acquaintance from Echo's ball, a Lieutenant Averley, rushed up to her and begged to be allowed to join their group. If Lord Bell, she thought, had indeed been obliged to find one of his own friends, it might have been someone who was privy to his improper pursuit of Sophia; she had no idea of what gentlemen talked about when they went off by themselves, and imagined that ribald exchanges of conquests were common. But thanks to the young military man, who was oblivious of any intrigue, and the gallant efforts of Lady Amarantha to maintain the conversation at an innocuous and sparkling level, the ensuing supper wasn't painful, though Lord Bell passed the entire time leering at Sophia, except when his sense of fairness demanded he ogle Lady Amarantha or her daughter.

Echo who, with her Spanish count, rounded out their party, was also a great diversion. Sophia and

Amarantha were much amused in watching the pretty
lures that Echo seemed to feel honour-bound to cast
out to Averley. Finally the young man, quite torn between the lovely debutante and her older friend, Miss
Dalrymple, assuaged his confused sense of disloyalty
by bringing both ladies an inordinate amount of re-
freshments, which behaviour Echo found nearly irresistible.

As Sophia sipped her second glass of champagne—
fetched for her by the solicitous lieutenant, who then
hurried off in search of more lemonade for Echo—
Lord Bell finally seized the moment for a private word
with his cousin. Lady Amarantha had dropped her
vigilance to essay her rudimentary knowledge of
Spanish with the count, Miss Burroughs's attention
was all given to her plate, the lieutenant had not yet
returned with the latest load of victuals, so the time
was right. "Fair Sophia," the baron whispered, leaning toward her so that their shoulders touched, "I delight in finding you so quiet and circumspect tonight.
It wouldn't do to cause talk—yet."

Sophia stared. "What can you be referring to, sir?"
she asked in feigned innocence. Her blush, however,
was eloquent in its perfect appraisal of his lordship's
innuendo.

"Yes, Bell, what the devil *are* you referring to?
Please to repeat your remark—some of us didn't hear
it," said a familiar, good-humoured voice from behind Sophia's chair. She turned to see Lord Carrisbrooke and couldn't help breaking out in a smile of
relief at his appearance.

Lord Bell frowned. "Nothing important; something about, er, the lady's and my mutual kin," he invented, with a proprietary glance at Sophia that

bespoke a relation's right to talk to her however he liked. "You weren't meant to hear it, Carrisbrooke," he added in resentment. His blue eyes narrowed as he surveyed the handsome marquis, standing so comfortably behind the chair of his own intended paramour. Remarking a certain something in the man's attitude, Lord Bell screwed up his eyes even more until they were no more than sharp blue slits. Dash it all, she was his cousin, and it was only right that he have first claim to giving her a *carte blanche*.

Carrisbrooke bowed in acknowledgement of Bell's words. Then he turned to greet the other members of the little group.

"You told me you wouldn't be caught dead here, brother," Lady Amarantha said frankly. "Has your interest in music revived, then?"

"My respect for music was what made me decline initially, Amarantha," responded Carrisbrooke, his eyes twinkling. "But I chanced to be passing and thought you ladies could use a chaperon. I see I was right; the three of you no sooner get out of my sight than you're cavorting with more men than I can count." His jovial words and bright smile couldn't give offence; and it was certainly delightful to see him, as his sister and his niece hastened to assure the irreverent marquis.

"But you can count three, Uncle, and that's how many men we have," added the methodical Echo. "Four, with you."

"Merely on my way through the room, Niece," said Carrisbrooke with a wave of his hand. Then, in direct negation of his words, he pulled a frail gilt chair from a nearby corner, placed it between Sophia and Lord Bell, then seated himself with a flourish. "I've no more than fifteen minutes at the very most to spend with all of you. Now, young Echo,'' he said, turning once more to the fairylike creature in pale pink muslin, ''tell me about your conquests of this evening.''

Echo gave a serious nod. ''Well, Uncle Charles, this isn't a ball or anything of that sort. We have had to sit quite still to listen to music. So I haven't made any conquests except for Count Almirez, and I had him already.''

Here the count, who had been listening along with the rest of the group to this artless speech, interrupted to assure his fair one that he was indeed at her feet.

''Yes,'' Echo said, accepting his compliment matter-of-factly, ''and Lieutenant Averley has been most attentive to both me and Sophia. But it's difficult in general to cast out lures at an affair of this sort.''

At which the company had no choice but to burst out laughing.

Under cover of the general hilarity, Carrisbrooke made bold to whisper to Sophia, ''You are looking lovely tonight, my dear.'' He gave an approving glance at her costume of ice-blue sarcenet trimmed with white lace, a gown Amarantha had tossed aside as much too *jeune fille* for herself, but perfect for the younger Sophia.

Sophia nodded shortly, casting a terrified look at Lord Bell, which Carrisbrooke intercepted.

''I've just told your cousin she looks lovely tonight, Bell,'' he said loudly.

''Quite,'' responded Bell in a cold voice, holding his quizzing glass aloft. He was by now certain that he had a rival of some sort in this outrageous marquis.

Carrisbrooke was no less certain of which way the land lay in the matter of Sophia and her erstwhile cousin. The baron's leering attentions were testimony to the fact that he meant to ensnare the lady in some way, and knowing Bell's proclivities Carrisbrooke didn't hesitate to think the worst.

Lord Bell, a widower, had married in his youth, and his heir was safely tucked away at Eton by this time; thus he had no need to beget legitimate children. The baron's widowhood, rumour had it, had been pleasantly passed in the company of one member of the muslin set after another, though he was also not above seducing the occasional respectable lady, nor frequenting the seedier houses of pleasure in the notorious area surrounding Covent Garden. Now, audacious though it was, the baron no doubt planned to seduce his eminently respectable cousin, Miss Dalrymple. As Carrisbrooke thought with a smile of his own plans for Sophia, he determined that his foiling of Bell's little plot must be amusing as well as effective.

These two rival cavaliers faced off in a nearly invisible way while Sophia struggled with her various feelings of embarrassment, elation and confusion. It was horrid that Carrisbrooke was quizzing Lord Bell in that strange way, and at her expense; but it was pure pleasure to see him. However, her anxiety to hide that pleasure and thus any sign that she loved the marquis was spoiling what would otherwise have been the high point of her evening.

And why conceal it? she asked herself sharply. Wouldn't the expression of her acknowledged love make their proposed liaison even more pleasant than Carrisbrooke already thought it would be? Perhaps so, perhaps not, from a gentleman's viewpoint—Sophia really had no idea—but from her side it would be unthinkably difficult. She was not at all certain that the marquis, if he knew that her sentiments for him had flowered into the most tender, might not pity her. This would be bad enough. What she was loath to see was his continued adherence to their "bargain" in the face of her love. He might not think it dishonourable to take her affection as casually as he now planned to take her body! And such behaviour on his part would hurt Sophia most dreadfully, for she had discovered—and perhaps always known—that her body and her love were two very distinct and separate things. It would break her heart if Carrisbrooke accepted the one as casually and lightly as she had requested he accept the other. Thus she would not allow it.

While Sophia thought along these lines, presenting a very grave and angelic appearance as she did so, her prospective seducers continued to spar—in an adroit and urbane way, of course. "Miss Dalrymple, despite her elegant and frivolous appearance in that very becoming gown, is quite a serious young woman," said Carrisbrooke with a raking glance at the item of clothing in question. Sophia blushed.

"Serious indeed," intoned Lord Bell.

"She has told me she can't wait to return to her rural parish, where she does nothing but run back and forth between her duties at the church and vicarage and the cottages of the more indigent of my tenants. This isn't to discount the invaluable contribution she makes to the local dame school," continued the marquis.

Sophia stared in surprise. She had had no idea that the great Lord Carrisbrooke, so occupied with concerns of government and estate as she knew him to be despite his lack of seriousness in this intrigue with herself, was at all cognizant of her activities.

"Invaluable," said Bell with a cough. "As her relation, I must beg you, Carrisbrooke, to give over praising the young lady to the skies in her own presence. You're embarrassing her."

"Indeed, I can't but agree with the baron," put in Amarantha, who had been looking on with interest for some minutes.

Sophia smiled rather weakly as her own contribution, for she found herself unable to venture a word. She felt that her voice might shake, if not with merriment then some other emotion.

Carrisbrooke favoured his two critics—and Sophia—with his most dazzling smile. "Ah, far be it from me to cause the lady any discomfort, now or—" with a tender look at Sophia that infuriated both her and Lord Bell, for very different reasons "—at any time in the future. And now, Miss Dalrymple, may I offer you my arm for a turn around the room?"

"Do go on, my dear, I'll take care of your cousin," advised Lady Amarantha coolly, with an effort to hide the matchmaking zeal which had begun to creep into all her dealings with her friend and her irrepressible brother. In a considerable lessening of her usual *froideur* toward Lord Bell, she then laid a gloved hand upon this gentleman's arm and begged him to tell her what he had thought of the musical performance just past.

Lord Bell was thus obliged to remain and seethe by the chair of her ladyship for the moment, rather than springing to Sophia's other side as he had intended a moment before.

Sophia, for her part, had to stand up and lay her hand within the marquis's crooked arm, and then move sedately away from the others. As the two retreated down the long supper room in the general direction of the music salon, Sophia couldn't help overhearing Echo ingenuously informing Almirez that Uncle had quite a *tendre* for Miss Dalrymple, didn't he think so? They were mercifully out of earshot of the count's reply.

"A very pretty colour in your cheeks tonight, my love," said Carrisbrooke in a low voice. "My sweet niece is not in league with me to put you to the blush, I do assure you."

"As you say," Sophia contested as mildly as she could, noting with dismay the interest various of the other guests seemed to be exhibiting toward herself and her escort.

"Perhaps Echo only sees what all the world does," mused the marquis, directing his eyes to a point somewhere above Sophia's head in a falsely innocent look that did not fool Miss Dalrymple in the least.

"My lord," she made herself say with proper severity, in as quiet a voice as she could manage, for the press of bejewelled ladies and elegant gentlemen who surrounded them didn't allow for true conversation, "you must have some particular intelligence for me, or I'm sure you wouldn't have exposed me in this way, by taking me off from the others."

"What?" The marquis stared incredulously. "My dear young woman, if I see one pair of desultory strollers in this company, I see a dozen. Who doesn't feel the need for exercise after such an evening of sitting down as you've just spent?"

"And which you didn't, since you got here only a moment ago," Sophia reminded him.

"Yes. Well, let's find a corner somewhere and I'll tell you what I have to say, for you're in the right of it as usual, my love. There is a particular intelligence," Lord Carrisbrooke continued serenely, nodding to an acquaintance here and there as he strolled through the throng.

Knowing what his behaviour was wont to be in corners, and moreover very disturbed by his casual way of addressing her as his "love," Sophia couldn't repress a deep, resigned sigh.

The marquis patted her hand "No need to worry, my own. I'm not going to bite you," he said with a chuckle. He steered the way to the hall, where he was certain a small alcove would be available for his purposes.

The spot he remembered from previous intrigues was tenanted this evening by two giggling debutantes and their callow young cavaliers, all four whispering together in the most charmingly innocent, unchaperoned manner. The youngsters quailed before the forbidding stare of the marquis of Carrisbrooke, and in a trice the room was clear. Carrisbrooke handed Sophia into the alcove, drew the concealing curtains closed and embraced her immediately in what she was coming to think of as his normal manner. By an effort of will Sophia didn't allow herself to cling to him in the least, and sensing her unwillingness, he soon released her.

"Your pardon, my dear, for the folly of laying hands on you in a place where we might easily be observed," muttered Carrisbrooke, as with gallant attention he kissed Sophia chastely on the forehead,

settled her on the brocade sofa which graced the alcove and took a relaxed stance before her. "Overcome by your charms as usual. You look very
beautiful. Now! I've brought you here to warn you
about Lord Bell."

Sophia reacted with a mixture of pleasure and resentment. "About my cousin?" she asked in a cool
voice.

"Yes. The man means to seduce you. He has no
need to marry again, and if he did, he'd go with an
heiress," the marquis informed her in the stern manner of a careful guardian.

Sophia let a laugh escape her. It was so strange to be
warned by one seducer about the intentions of another. "I have Lord Bell well in hand," she assured
Carrisbrooke.

He stared at her. "You speak as though he'd already made his indecent overtures. Surely he hasn't
dared; he's barely met you."

Sophia's lips twitched as she admitted, "He was so
obliging as to offer me his patronage for my book on
the very day we met."

"He wasn't!" Sophia could tell from the tone of the
marquis's voice that he had a very clear understanding of what Lord Bell's terms of patronage must have
been.

"Oh, yes, and to preserve my anonymity and yours,
sir, I had to tell him that I'd burned my manuscript."
Sophia smiled at the memory of her ruse. "But he
does still seem to think that I, well, need a protector.
I do want you to be assured, my lord," she finished,
looking earnestly at her companion, "that the unrav-
elling of this particular tangle is no concern of yours."

He frowned. "You mean to say that our relationship, being unsanctioned by the world, doesn't allow me to protect you? You're out there, my love. When you sold yourself to me you placed yourself under my protection. Whether you like it or not, I might add."

Sophia sighed. "But how absurd. Nothing is going to happen between me and Lord Bell—"

"You may be sure of that," snapped the marquis.

"And on the off chance that it did, what would you do? Call him out? Heavens, knowing what you know, my honour can never be in question," she continued in vexation.

"That remains to be seen. Watch yourself," said Carrisbrooke. Then, with no warning, he drew her to her feet once more and held her closely against his chest. "One kiss," he whispered, "and back you go to my sister; and I warn you I won't have my place usurped by your whoring rakeshame of a cousin. Excuse my language." And his lips came down on Sophia's in a kiss to which she couldn't help responding, though she tried to remain calm.

When he released her she leaned against him momentarily. "I . . ." she began before she could stop herself. Then, just in time, she bit back the confession of love that had nearly escaped her.

"You what?" murmured Carrisbrooke.

She remained silent, cursing her lack of control and trying to think of something else to substitute for the forbidden words. Thinking back on their conversation, she came up with a plausible substitute. "I wish you wouldn't say I sold myself," she improvised, much more quietly than such a complaint warranted.

He smiled down into her frightened eyes. "But why should my favourite authoress mince words? You did,'' he stated, and gave his familiar, wicked-sounding laugh.

Sophia nodded. "I know. But I still wish you wouldn't say so," she persisted, looking at the ground.

"It shall be as you wish," said Carrisbrooke with a bow. He offered his arm.

As they left the alcove to begin the walk back to the supper room, neither one of them remarked the sinister figure of Lord Bell, lurking behind a pillar and giving the impression of one who has just heard something much to his advantage.

CHAPTER TWELVE

ON THE MORNING after his interesting conversation with Sophia Dalrymple in that antechamber at Lady Sefton's, Lord Carrisbrooke arose much earlier than was his wont and summoned his secretary, the efficient Mr. Mudgely, to attend him in the breakfast parlour.

This virtuous young man, who had risen at dawn as he usually did, tramped briskly about in the morning air for an hour before his Spartan breakfast, and been busying himself with Carrisbrooke's correspondence for quite two hours, very correctly left his small office as soon as he got the message. The secretary was naturally curious at the unprecedented order.

"My lord?" Mr. Mudgely bowed before the marquis, who was attacking a large plate of kidneys and steak with nearly as much enthusiasm as his ethereal niece would have brought to the operation.

"Mudgely, you haven't been my secretary for long, but I've grown to admire your discretion and your astute ways in the short time we've been associated," said Carrisbrooke affably, motioning the young man to a chair.

Mr. Mudgely sat down nervously. Although he did dine with the family on the very rare occasions they spent the evening at home, he was still somewhat reluctant to take his ease in the presence of a nobleman and military hero of Carrisbrooke's stature. "Thank you, my lord," he said in carefully bland response to the marquis's compliments, which had caused a secret thrill in his manly breast.

"No, it's I who thank you, for the service," replied Carrisbrooke. It might have been noted that his eyes were gleaming with humour. "I have a special assignment for you today, something out of the ordinary, and I'm convinced you'll handle it with your usual efficiency and in all of the secrecy I require."

Mr. Mudgely's eyes widened. "Yes, my lord," he answered calmly. Secrecy! Mudgely's activities on behalf of the marquis of Carrisbrooke had so far been confined to the most ordinary of correspondence, research and message carrying. There had been a few confidential missives to be delivered to other members of Parliament, but nothing in the least way irregular. And he knew from other men of his occupation that noble employers often did have havey-cavey dealings of one sort or another in which they made use of their secretaries. The prospect was exciting. Carrisbrooke was finally showing himself to be less the business-oriented paragon and more the hardened, ruthless libertine whom Mudgely had halfway hoped to encounter in his first foray into the world of politics and intrigue. "You may rely on me in all things, Lord Carrisbrooke," added the young man.

"It's quite a simple matter," stated the marquis, a glint still in his dark eyes. "I want a particular gentleman's activities monitored. I want him watched night and day, in effect, and I rely upon you to hire suitable spies to do this, and to forward word to myself, through said spies, of anything untoward in this man's movements. I'm going out of Town shortly—today in fact—and I want to be certain that I hear by each post all the details of how this person conducts himself. Do you understand?''

Mudgely, with all the unflappable dignity which was to stand him in good stead in years to come, nodded. "Yes, my lord.''

"And can you arrange to have the man in question watched round the clock? You have the necessary contacts? If you do not, I'm sure some of my friends commonly involve themselves in this sort of thing and could direct you to the proper quarter.''

"I'm certain I can find out from one of *my* friends where such people are to be hired, sir,'' said Mudgely confidently. "Members of the ton do often have each other watched—grounds for divorce, and so forth— and I have several acquaintances who are, like myself, in service in great houses.''

"Yes, quite. Well, proceed then with the utmost caution and discretion. Here, on this sheet of paper, is the name of my quarry. See you do not speak it aloud.'' And Carrisbrooke handed to his interested employee a sheet of his notepaper, folded twice, on which was written in his most flourishing hand the name of Lord Bell.

As Mudgely was pocketing the paper the door opened and Miss Dalrymple came in. Both gentlemen sprang to their feet.

"Madam, I didn't realize you were such an early riser,'' said Carrisbrooke with his most engaging grin. "No, don't retreat,'' he added, for Sophia was showing definite signs of leaving the room as suddenly as she had come. "Mudgely and I have finished our business, and I my breakfast. We are both off, and we leave you, though reluctantly, to a solitary meal.'' His eyes flashed mischievously. "I will hope to see you later in the morning, though. Shall we say eleven?"

Sophia, who by now could have refused him nothing and was finding that her knees were annoyingly weak at the mere sight of the man, nodded her assent.

"Servant, madam," murmured Mr. Mudgely, then discreetly left the room. His expressionless face did not betray whether he thought privacy was warranted between the lady and the marquis, or whether he was merely in a hurry to do his lordship's bidding.

"The man has providentially left us alone, but I'll not take advantage," said Carrisbrooke, holding a chair for Sophia. She tamely sat. "I'll let that wait till eleven. In the library." He chuckled in his affected, wicked way, bowed and left Sophia to a solitary contemplation of her coffee cup and a pleasurable dread of what the late-morning interview might bring.

Now that his commission for Mr. Mudgely was set well in train, the marquis felt free to proceed to the next matter of business. Going out, he mounted his curricle, a fashionable and dashing vehicle in bronze trimmed with gold and drawn by his favourite pair of high-stepping bays, and directed his cattle to Messrs Rundell and Bridge, jewellers, on Ludgate Hill. There he picked up an item which occasioned its share of comment from the staff of the establishment and the few early-rising members of the *beau monde* who observed him. There were a few other trifling stops he had to make during the course of the morning, but he was back in Grosvenor Square shortly before eleven.

While the marquis went about his errands, Sophia passed the morning in an agony over her vexing feelings of affection for the infuriating man. A couple of hours spent turning over the leaves of her novel did nothing to calm her nor to turn her from the course she had awakened that morning determined to follow. Yes, she was decided. She would confess her embarrassing love for the marquis to his handsome and teasing face, and see what happened. Maybe he would chivalrously insist on not seducing her; maybe he would laugh, and kill her affection forever. But she had to know. By the time the library door opened, at exactly eleven by the clock on the mantelpiece, she was quite nervous.

Carrisbrooke therefore beheld a very perturbed-looking lady, who clutched in her white-knuckled hands a certain calf-bound volume. He smiled at her distress.

"Ah, how goes it?" he asked jovially, advancing to the Windsor chair in which Miss Dalrymple had seated herself and taking the one opposite. "Has Murray done his work well?"

Sophia gave a weak smile. "The worst thing I've found yet, aside from several tiny errors of print, is one place in volume 3 where two sentences are made into one. But on the whole it's a beautiful job." She closed the book and cast down her eyes in an excess of embarrassment at what she had to say to the marquis before she left the room.

"Well, then." Carrisbrooke beamed and reached over to pat Sophia chastely on the hand. "I've asked you here to inform you I'm leaving Town."

"Indeed?" Sophia's reply sounded cold and dry to her own ears. She was having trouble controlling her voice at all, given the fact that she must somehow approach the subject of her tender feelings for the marquis. She wondered in an irritated way why, of all times, he hadn't simply burst into the room and laid hands on her as he usually did. A confession such as she had in mind would be much more easily uttered to his coatfront.

"Yes. As I told you last night, I find it necessary to arrange privately for our future association."

Sophia smiled at him as lightly as she could. "You mean to say you're going to rent a love nest or some such?" At the expression on his face, she said, "My lord, it's you who told me not to mince words."

"You authors, always taking people literally," said Carrisbrooke in a hearty tone. "Now, if you please, you are to utter pretty phrases about how you'll miss me. I won't be gone long, though. I assume it will be merely a matter of a few days."

"Of course the other ladies and I will feel the lack of your presence," said Sophia primly. "Not to say your protection."

Carrisbrooke thought with a smug smile of the morning's interview with Mudgely, in which he had tried to ensure Sophia's safety in one way at least. "Come now, is that any way for a paramour to talk?" he said in a rallying tone. "A tender word or two is part of the game, my dear."

Sophia cast down her eyes. "I'll miss you," she began quietly and was trying to screw up her courage to utter the next words. She had decided upon "because I love you" when she was forestalled by Carrisbrooke patting her hand again.

"Excellent. Now I have a little token for you to remember me by." He took a small velvet box from his pocket and placed it in the lady's lap. He waited expectantly, and Sophia realized that she was expected to open the box now. She further realized that the package no doubt contained some trinket such as might be given to a mistress. The thought depressed her.

"My lord, I have no need for gifts," she protested, opening the box as she spoke the words. Her next utterance was a gasp of astonishment, for there, reposing on a bed of black velvet, was the largest diamond she had ever seen in her life.

"Take it out," urged Carrisbrooke. "It's set in a ring."

But Sophia couldn't even bring herself to touch the flashing stone. "My dear sir, I could never keep this," she said, miserably shaking her head and inspiring in the marquis a desire, with difficulty suppressed, to take her in his arms and laugh away her reluctance.

"Why not?"

"Well, because it's such a very... it makes me feel just like a Cyprian," sighed Sophia. "Which I am, or will be, and I know it's by my choice, so you needn't plague me. But I could never show this to anyone, or wear it, and it would be much better if you didn't give me gifts."

"You might wear it for me, in private," suggested the marquis smoothly, putting into Sophia's head visions of wild bacchanalian scenes in which she would be hung with jewellery and nothing else.

"I simply can't accept it," she insisted. She snapped the box shut and held it out to the marquis with an appealing glance. Strangely, she found herself altogether cured of the desire to confess her love to this man, for suddenly her feelings were once again a secret he must never guess. The instant change of heart was due to this very calculating way in which her prospective lover had chosen to put her in her place, she was sure.

The marquis refused to take the box and set it firmly back in Sophia's lap. There was a little more wrangling back and forth, which ended when Carrisbrooke threatened to go to Sophia's bedroom and place it under her pillow if she didn't take it like a good girl. Finally, under the threat of this impropriety, she had to concede.

"That's settled, at least," said Carrisbrooke with a sly but engaging grin. "You might find this easier to bear, my dear—this being given jewellery, I mean—if I assure you that it's part of my usual way with the ladies, and thus a strict part of our agreement."

Sophia nodded, resolving to hide the embarrassing ring in the darkest corner of her bedroom. "Yes, of course I know that the Fashionable Impures at the opera and in the Park seem to be well supplied with this sort of thing." She tapped the lid of the box and gave an inward shudder. Then she managed to smile impishly up at Carrisbrooke. "Tell me, do you think my cousin Lord Bell would have been as generous?"

"That, my dear, you will never know," said Carrisbrooke with a firm nod of his head and a stern look that was quite spoiled when he broke into another irrepressible smile.

Sophia had to return the smile, and their eyes met in a moment of perfect understanding of the probable vagaries of Lord Bell.

"Now, my love," said the marquis, rising from his chair, "I must leave you. I plan to be gone on my way within the hour, and I must make my *adieux* to Amarantha and the child. By the way, I'm saying that urgent estate business has called me out of Town at this time. Don't give me away." He chuckled.

"Your lordship knows I would be the last person in the world to do anything so cork-brained," replied Sophia with spirit. "But would it be so horrid if the ton should get wind that you're readying a love nest? Never mind for whom; of course I would never give *that* out."

The marquis frowned. To Sophia's mind he positively glowered at her, and she realized that when he frowned his eyebrows came together in an alarming way. It struck her that she had hardly ever seen him do anything but smile.

"Yes, it would be horrid," he said shortly. "But I know that you're only funning, and you'll hold your tongue. After all, you are a clergyman's daughter, and a clergyman's daughter is the soul of honour."

Sophia bowed in acknowledgement of this ambiguous compliment.

Carrisbrooke next reached for her hand and held it briefly to his lips in as formal a salute as she had ever had from him. "Goodbye, my dear," he said in a gentle voice. "I'll be back soon, and all will be well." And not pausing for any reply, he turned and left the room.

Sophia looked after him in astonishment. He had actually managed a whole interview without kissing her! And his remarks about the secrecy they must maintain on the subject of his business in the country were wildly out of character. Was the man belatedly developing a puritan sense of middle-class respectability?

CHAPTER THIRTEEN

IT WAS PERHAPS TO BE EXPECTED that Sophia's cozy fortress of anonymous authorship would come crashing down around her sooner or later when she was betrayed by some well-meaning soul as the authoress of *The River Garden*. However, anyone would have thought she might have had more than a couple of days to enjoy her secret. Unfortunately, this was not to be.

On the very day after Lord Carrisbrooke's departure for an uncertain destination, Lady Amarantha found herself entertaining a superfluity of morning callers. This was in the usual course of events, naturally, since Echo was now "out" and cutting quite a dash; and indeed fully half of the callers were very young men who were exhibiting the normal fawning qualities of males in love. But there were also many ladies. In fact, on this particular morning two of the patronesses of Almack's, Lady Jersey and Mrs. Drummond-Burrell, had called for the express purpose of presenting Echo and her mama with cards for the weekly subscription ball at that august institution. Besides these formidable ladies, several elderly dowagers, engaged in collecting and dispersing gossip, were sprinkled about the drawing room where Lady Amarantha was receiving. Then there was her particular friend, Lady Stephens, and all the young men, not excepting the Count Almirez, who were grouped about Echo like bees round a flower. Miss Dalrymple was also in evidence this morning, busy in a corner of the room detailing a complicated receipt for anti-rheumatic tea to one of the oldest of the ladies.

Lady Stephens, a great reader, had been to Hatchard's that morning and picked up a new novel. "I hear that it's by a lady who wishes for a particular reason to be mysterious," she said chattily to Amarantha, "and that your brother, my dear, is somehow concerned. In fact, he's said to be the hero. I have it here in my bag. Yes, *The River Garden*."

Lady Amarantha nodded cheerfully and said that she'd heard of the book, too. In fact, she was also reading it. She was amused at this evidence that Murray had obviously been puffing the work that way, though he had told Charles he would not, and she wasn't at all displeased at the thought that dear Sophia's novel was to be sought after because of a supposed mystery concerning Carrisbrooke. Amarantha was sure that the book could stand on its own merit, but the great thing was to get it read. She looked forward with pleasure to a spirited discussion of the novel with Lydia Stephens, when that lady finished with it, and she glanced fondly at Sophia, who was still expounding on the theme of some medicine to that depressing Mrs. Calvert.

Then it happened. "Oh," said Echo, lifting her exquisitely curly blonde head and fixing honest blue eyes on the book in Lady Stephens's hands, "Miss Dalrymple wrote that."

A momentary silence followed Miss Burroughs's shocking pronouncement, while all eyes turned immediately to the demure Miss Dalrymple, whose voice, now recommending a strong poultice of mint leaves as a cure for the headache, was suddenly the most audible in the room.

Sophia cut herself off in midsentence and looked up, startled by the sudden stillness of the room. It seemed as though dozens of bright, birdlike eyes were fixed on her. Nervously she glanced down at her dress, sure that at the very least her bosom had somehow broken free from her quietly coloured poplin bodice; but everything seemed to be fastened.

"How interesting!" said Lady Jersey. "*The River Garden*! Why, I'm halfway through the second volume, for Murray recommended it to me and brought me a copy. Such talent, Miss Dalrymple." And this powerful arbitress of the ton decided on the spot to get the authoress a ticket to the next subscription ball at her King Street stronghold; she hadn't brought one today, as neither she nor the other patronesses of Almack's had thought this country nobody worthy of admittance to those august rooms. There had been no danger of rudeness to the Burroughs ladies in excluding their friend, for Lady Amarantha was always saying that her guest wished to live very quietly. But Sally Jersey was shrewd. She knew that this retiring country spinster was about to cause a sensation, given the subject of her novel. An unimportant country girl of mature years who married an earl whose description was almost exactly that of Carrisbrooke? There was a good joke here, at the very least.

One of the other ladies mentioned that she would go instantly to Hatchard's to purchase Miss Dalrymple's little work, though she didn't as a rule look into novels, for it was something new to her to be acquainted with an authoress. A general conversation broke out again, and many words of congratulation were directed at Sophia for her sly coup. While Sophia's face got redder and redder, Lady Amarantha was wishing she could take a strap to her wayward daughter. And Echo, knowing only that she had satisfied her mama's friend's curiosity on a very minor point, continued to chatter to her masculine admirers.

When the room was finally cleared much later in the morning, Amarantha turned to Echo and said very fiercely, "Didn't you know, Miss, that Sophia's writing that book was to be a secret?"

Echo's large eyes opened wide. "Why, no, Mama. Was it?"

Sophia had calmed down somewhat from her initial panicked wish to hide in the very corner of her armoire in which she had secreted Carrisbrooke's diamond ring, and she broke in to say, "I don't believe we did tell Echo about the secret, my lady. She didn't know she was doing anything I shouldn't like."

Amarantha sighed. "Yes, but, oh, my dear, I know how important your anonymity was to you."

Sophia managed a bright smile. "There is always my next book," she said in a light tone. "Nobody will notice this one, in particular. You'll see. It's only a simple little story, nothing in the style of *Childe Harold* or anything of Mr. Scott's, and I'm certainly not a person of importance in the *beau monde*. Who will care that I wrote a novel?" These words were spoken mainly to convince herself.

"Yes, but—" Amarantha bit back her next words. She had been about to do something quite unnecessary, which was mention to Sophia that people were bound to think the fictional earl of Connaught was the

marquis of Carrisbrooke, and that therefore Sophia
must be Olivia, the heroine. But better let the girl lin-
ger in ignorance as long as possible, and Amarantha
would think of some way to scotch any such imperti-
nent tittle-tattle before it reached Sophia's ears.

"But what, my lady?" Sophia was saying serenely,
for the more she thought about it, the more certain she
became that a mild, domestic novel such as she had
written would never be noticed by the haut ton.

Amarantha sighed. "But you'd better resign yourself to going to Almack's," she improvised. "Sally
Jersey left with what some of us call her patroness's
leer. A lust which is not for things corporeal, but
rather for something new to talk about, and a new
person to take up."

"Oh, dear," exclaimed Sophia in true distress. It
had never been one of her ambitions to make an appearance at Almack's, the notorious marriage mart
where scores of hopeful debutantes were paraded each
spring. It would be ridiculous for one of her advanced age to join in the husband hunt, and she knew
she wasn't quite old and imposing enough to be a
chaperon. However, she reminded herself sternly, as
a writer she must grasp at new experiences whenever
she could.

Echo was prattling on about how Sophia would no
doubt love Almack's, as would she, and detailing
which white gown she intended to wear on the next
Wednesday evening, when they were to present themselves. The talk turned to the all-important theme of
what cut-down, refurbished ensemble of Lady Amarantha's would best become Miss Dalrymple.

AMARANTHA'S INTERPRETATION of Sally Jersey's mien had been accurate. A card for Sophia did arrive, commanding her presence at Almack's. Therefore, at ten o'clock on the Wednesday evening, a mere two days after Echo's disclosure—two days which Sophia had spent unblushingly in the privacy of her room whenever guests were present in Grosvenor Square, pleading the headache and cursing her own timidity—the obscure Miss Dalrymple found herself entering the sacred rooms in King Street and making her curtsey to the lionesses who guarded the sanctuary: Lady Jersey, Lady Cowper, Countess Lieven and Mrs. Drummond-Burrell. They none of them bothered to suppress the amused interest they felt on seeing Sophia.

She knew that she was in her best looks. Nervousness had given her delicate complexion a high colour which was most becoming, if almost feverish; and she had on a gown of Italian crepe in a most fetching shade of pale lilac, which she knew was very flattering. This gave her the confidence to hold her head—in the version of the Meduse at which Amarantha's dresser was becoming quite adept—very high indeed.

She was aware that this would be no ordinary evening, and that it was quite possible that someone might ask her about her book. She had memorized several vague and commonplace things to say if such an incident occurred. But she definitely did not expect her cousin, Lord Bell, to solicit her hand as soon as she was announced and lead her off to the next set without even pausing to wait for her reply.

Sophia gave Lady Amarantha a stricken look as she was borne away, for Amarantha had assured her Bell was never admitted to Almack's. Neither of the ladies could know that the baron, hearing that Miss Dalrymple was to grace the rooms that evening, had managed to worm his way into the sanctuary by dint of a series of extravagant compliments to ladies Jersey and Cowper the day before in Bond Street.

"Quite a dark horse, aren't you, my dear?" murmured Bell as they took their places in the set. "Burned, indeed."

Sophia smiled apologetically, but said nothing. She had understood his reference at once, but she couldn't think of a single excuse for her lie.

Conversation was necessarily stilted between her and her cousin, thanks to the varied movements demanded by the quadrille, but it did not take much interaction for Sophia to collect that her noble relation was quite overset, not to say raging mad, at her audacious behaviour in refusing his patronage, his *carte blanche* and—if she were to credit his dramatic dagger glances and mutterings of distress—his regard. She didn't believe anything but his pride was wounded and considered it very odd in any case that a man of his superior understanding would not know that a respectable spinster without protectors in Town must try any ruse to save herself from the clutches of such a wicked nobleman as he. She hoped to have a chance to explain as much to Lord Bell, in a way which would flatter his vanity and not insult him, and to regain her original place with the man: that is to say, a distant relation who had no claim upon her and of whom he had no thoughts whatsoever. The dance ended, and Lord Bell gave his arm to escort Sophia back to Amarantha.

"Playing me and Carrisbrooke off against each other, are you?" said the baron through his teeth. "You'll catch cold at that little game, my dear."

"Sir," asked Sophia quietly, "what has Lord Carrisbrooke to do with this sudden turn you have for being vexed with me?"

"What indeed?" snarled her cousin. "Do you really hope to rivet the man tighter than you already have? I warn you, he's not any more apt than the rest of us to make an unsuitable marriage."

Sophia's eyebrows lifted quizzically. Marriage! If he only knew what her real position was with Carrisbrooke. But it struck her with a sudden clarity that her cousin could only have picked up such a bacon-brained notion from one source: he must have read, and misinterpreted, her novel! Certainly Carrisbrooke's manners to her in real life had always been rakish but satirical, as they were to most women. There had been nothing to warrant speculations as to her designs on him, except—and she had uneasily wondered about this more than once, silly thought though it was—that the earl of her novel did look quite a bit like the marquis, and her heroine was in a situation rather similar to her own. There was nothing in it, of course. Everyone thought she had written the novel before meeting Carrisbrooke, didn't they? And if she had invented an ideal man who accidentally resembled the marquis, it wasn't her fault.

"The real world isn't like one of those lending library novels that you ladies read—and write—so avidly," continued Lord Bell in a cold voice, putting Sophia into a gilt chair at the sidelines. He superciliously raised his quizzing glass to observe that a herd of witless males were immediately flocking to his cousin's vicinity. "I believe you'll regret not accepting my patronage, my dear. Had you sold yourself to *me*, you might at least have counted upon my discretion. *Adieu*." And with a mocking bow he took himself off to the card room, leaving Sophia speechless, for she could remember very well the only occasion on which the word "sold" had been bandied about in this connection. Carrisbrooke had used the term, and she had objected to it, that night at Lady Sefton's *musicale*! But Bell had certainly not been present. Her conjectures about the baron's having read her book were wrong, then. He had merely eavesdropped on her conversation with the marquis in that antechamber at Lady Sefton's! And though she couldn't for the life of her remember all that she and Carrisbrooke had said at that time, the secret of their prospective liaison had obviously been given away.

Sophia had to make all these connections silently, and in a moment's time, for she was being eagerly sought after for the next dance. In a rather distracted manner she gave her hand to Count Almirez, who, as she well knew, would only want to speak of Echo during the set, and what could be more innocuous and restful than such a conversation?

Sophia and the handsome young man went down the dance, and the lady's mind was running along totally different lines from her polite murmurs of "Yes, very beautiful," and "Quite charming, and such a delightfully frank manner." As the count stole burning glances at Echo and her current partner, a subaltern of very tender years, Sophia, wearing a thoughtful look, stared into space. Miss Dalrymple was very much afraid that her devoted kinsman wouldn't be silent about her conversation with Carrisbrooke; he had as much as told her so. She wished desperately for a confidant. Carrisbrooke *would* be out of Town! She toyed for a brief moment with the idea of telling Lady Amarantha the whole sordid story, but she couldn't consider such a course for long. Though she had every high opinion of the lady's broadmindedness and sense of humour, it would be too humiliating to admit to Amarantha that she had been harbouring a future courtesan who happened to be a very respectable vicar's daughter.

No, Sophia must bear this alone and stay out of the public eye as much as possible. And perhaps Lord Bell wasn't really going to be as odiously indiscreet as he had indicated; perhaps no one in the ton would care, in any case. It was such a tangle! Sophia sighed audibly, and the count, in the act of leading her back to Lady Amarantha, asked if he might do anything for her.

"Why, yes, you may dance with Echo again. It would give me such pleasure to see the two of you together," said Sophia with the best smile she could manage.

"Ah, Miss Dalrymple, you are an angel," exclaimed the dashing Spaniard. He kissed her hand with a flourish and rushed to do her bidding.

Sophia didn't stay at the side of Lady Amarantha for more than a moment, and she didn't sit out one dance. In terms of social success, it was a very pleasant evening. When the waltz struck up, Lady Jersey, with Lieutenant Averley in tow, actually approached Miss Dalrymple and presented the young man as a most desirable partner. Sophia smiled and coloured at this. She, at nearly twenty-five, was being treated in the same way as a debutante, and it was gratifying, if a bit embarrassing. Never thinking to go to Almack's, she hadn't been excluding herself from the waltz at dances as young ladies usually did, pending the approval of the mighty patronesses, and it had been most kind of Lady Jersey to overlook that lapse.

It wouldn't have done to miss the waltzes this evening, Sophia thought as she whirled in Averley's arms and later in those of Almirez, for the quick pace and exercise were just what she needed to clear the cobwebs. In fact, she ended by enjoying those parts of the evening in which she could make herself forget Lord Bell and his shocking disclosure. She didn't see him again that evening. He either kept to the card room or had left without her notice.

"You have both had a *succès fou*," said Amarantha in the carriage going home. The glimmer from a street lamp revealed that she was looking at Sophia keenly as she spoke. "Did anyone talk to you about your book?" she added casually.

"Not precisely," answered Sophia, preferring to discount the ominous comments of Lord Bell. "Lady Jersey said some veiled thing I didn't quite understand, and of course Lady Stephens positively leered, but no one made specific mention of it."

"Good," said Amarantha thoughtfully. She herself had been bombarded with questions about Miss Dalrymple's fantasy world and Carrisbrooke's place in it, and she was still plotting on how best to put an end to such ill-natured and potentially hurtful gibble-gabble.

AFTER THE EVENING at Almack's, which had been somewhat in the nature of a royal command, Sophia declared her intention to live quietly and attend no more parties during the remainder of her stay in Town, which, she said firmly, would end in a week.

"Oh, no," exclaimed Echo at the luncheon table, where this speech took place. "You simply can't bury yourself in the country again. How will you know if Almirez wins me or not?"

A peal of laughter broke from Sophia, and Lady Amarantha nearly choked on her tea. "My dear, what novel-slang!" said Sophia when she was able. "You must write me your news, of course. I really wish to go home, as Papa needs me there. But I've had a very enjoyable visit."

Amarantha sighed. "You mean you were having an enjoyable visit until this wretched child burst forth with your secret about *The River Garden*," she corrected. "Well, dear Sophia, I do think it would be difficult for you to go about if people choose to make your authorship food for gossip. And I'll warrant you won't listen to any arguments from me about the importance of pretending not to notice the cats, for you don't care for society. Isn't that so?"

Sophia looked up. In actual fact, she did feel a small stirring of heart at Lady Amarantha's cagey appeal to her pride.

"And furthermore," continued Amarantha, her shrewd dark eyes betraying that she knew her words had taken root, "did it never occur to you, dear, that people's interest in your writing will lead them to purchase the novel, and give you more of a nest egg for the future? If you merely crawl away in silence, people will think you a poor-spirited thing and not bother to rent it out at Hookham's, let alone purchase it at Hatchard's.

"You're much sought after—you've only to look at these," and Amarantha tapped with her forefinger the thick stack of invitations beside her plate, "to see your popularity. And these are just the ones delivered since breakfast! Go home if you must, Sophia, but I implore you not to make a hermit of yourself in the time remaining." Carrisbrooke's bride, thought Amarantha in determination, simply must hold her head up high during the little crisis to come. It would be excellent training for her future as a marchioness.

"Well, I know you're in the right of it, and I give over," said Sophia reasonably and after a moment's silence, during which the only noise in the room came from the crackling of the fire and the rhythmic click of Echo's fork on her plate of cold salmon—and this after all her mother's and Miss Helver's instructions and admonitions about how a lady never allows a sound from her cutlery!

"Of course I'm right, and you'll be glad one day," contested Lady Amarantha, breathing a sigh of relief. She had thought of a way, as it happened, to ensure that Sophia wouldn't be troubled much longer by snide comments on the subject of her novel. Amarantha sensed that such personal references were the only thing tormenting Sophia; for it was easy to tell that the young woman was proud enough of her literary work to own its authorship, and regretted merely that the novel's hero so closely resembled Carrisbrooke. "Now," Amarantha went on in a bracing tone, "what shall we all wear to this Venetian breakfast that the duchess is giving tomorrow? It sounds too *ennuyant*, my dears, but we dare not turn it down."

IT WAS AT THIS VERY BREAKFAST that Sophia, forth-rightly stylish in a jaconet muslin of a pale lemon colour and a broad-brimmed hat trimmed in matching ribbon, was tormented by the most serious social sniggering that she had as yet endured.

The first incident occurred when a gentleman asked her when he might wish her joy at her coming nuptials with Carrisbrooke. Since the speaker was a certain dandy whose reputation for snide comments was exceeded only by the legendary Brummell's, Sophia was first shocked, then dismayed that her personal life had taken on such prominence.

"Why, sir," she answered with wide-eyed blandness and an inward groan, "I cannot think what you mean."

The dandy leered. "Can you not, ma'am?" he responded in a languid, drawling tone. "Then I will not disturb you further. But do allow me to compliment your neatness of literary style." With that the provoking creature strolled off, leaving Sophia fuming and embarrassed.

The gentleman had no sooner gone on his way through the throng when his place was taken by Lady Russell, a crony of Lady Stephens, who was also quite ill-natured by repute and who also didn't hesitate to wish Miss Dalrymple joy, congratulating her in a very unpleasant way on snaring Carrisbrooke. Sophia outdid herself in seeming ignorance when she made her reply.

That evening she admitted to Lady Amarantha that the fortitude required of one in her situation was probably character building at its very best.

Lady Amarantha nodded, thinking of the bread she had cast upon the social waters herself that day, and whose return tenfold she expected before many hours passed.

"WELL, AMARANTHA," Lady Jersey said, sidling up to her friend in the press of people gathered in the duchess's saloons, "I confess myself to be quite muddled over this affair of Carrisbrooke and your little authoress friend from the country. Is it to be marriage, or did she accept a *carte blanche*, as her cousin Bell maintains? The girl is inscrutable, but she seems generally lacking in spirits. Is that only because Carrisbrooke is out of Town? Is the poor thing pining away?"

Lady Amarantha paled before this forthright assault, but she soon recovered both her complexion and her speech and was responding, in her most confidential tone, "Dearest Sally, my brother—and Sophia—wish for their understanding to remain private for the time being. He's gone out of Town to make some arrangements for the wedding; she is naturally perturbed that people seem to have found out the secret, for he adjured us all to keep it. But what is this ridiculous tale of a *carte blanche*? Bell must be mad, and raging with jealousy besides." She smiled. "Of course you *will* act surprised when you see the announcement in the *Gazette*, Sally? Charles does love surprises."

"MY DEAREST CREATURE," said Lady Jersey the very next evening, laying hold of Sophia's gloved arm as the latter paraded down the gallery at the opera on the arm of Lieutenant Averley, "I won't say a word. Trust me to keep the matter silent." Then the lady sailed away in the opposite direction.

"She *is* called Silence," remarked Averley, watching her ladyship drift down the corridor. "What is she keeping silent about this time, Miss Dalrymple?"

"I'm not certain," said Sophia, gazing after the lady also, and wondering mightily what had just taken place. But although Lady Jersey's words had been enigmatic, Sophia felt in that moment as if the worm had somehow turned as regarded her problems with ton gossip. This feeling was borne out in the ensuing days, when not one person alluded to her book except to praise its style, and no one mentioned Carrisbrooke to her at all. The fact that other, newer items of gossip had surfaced in society was not explanation enough.

No, someone must have put a word in Lady Jersey's ear, and thus in the ear of all the ton. But who had done it, and what had been said?

CHAPTER FOURTEEN

THE MARQUIS OF CARRISBROOKE opened the wicket gate in the simple privet hedge surrounding the vicarage garden. He had ridden up to Oakley Park direct from London—not an hour's journey on his fastest horse—but it had taken him a full evening of nervous pacing to get next door. It was morning now, he had just breakfasted, and his courage was high. He tapped on the door of the worn stone house and told the awed maidservant who answered his summons that he would speak to Mr. Dalrymple on a matter of urgent business.

The maid, in her nervousness, didn't think to inform the vicar first. Instead she immediately ushered the marquis into the library, where Mr. Dalrymple and his curate sat poring over some volumes of sermons.

"No, don't let me disturb you, vicar, Mr. . . . Penn, isn't it?" said Carrisbrooke in his most genial manner as the two clerics started out of their chairs like surprised mountain goats. "I need to have a word with Mr. Dalrymple, but it can wait. I see you're busy." And the marquis, feeling a return of his former trepidation, would have darted out of the room if the vicar hadn't insisted he stay.

"Mr. Penn can go into the parlour next door and continue to work on his sermon," suggested the vicar, with a commanding nod at his curate. "He's to speak

on Sunday, and I hope you're here to hear him, my
lord. We were just going over some texts on the subject of thrift."

"Yes, one of the seven deadly sins, isn't it?"
quipped the marquis before he could stop himself. He
then made a blundering apology that was received with
all kindness by Mr. Dalrymple, who knew the ways of
young sporting gentlemen, and icy coldness by Mr.
Penn, who immediately scooped up the books of sermons from the desk and proceeded, in high dudgeon,
into the parlour, firmly shutting the communicating
door.

"You must excuse Mr. Penn. He is very young and
very serious. He hasn't yet learned that humour is of
as much value in our profession as charity," said the
vicar jovially, his face breaking into a smile. "Will you
sit down, my lord? Shall I ask Dolly to bring us some
Madeira? Long ago your dear, lamented great-uncle
gave me a dozen bottles of his finest stock, so you
needn't fear that it will be undrinkable as the wines of
impecunious clergymen often are."

Carrisbrooke sat down and agreed wholeheartedly
to the idea of liquid refreshment. While the two men
waited for Dolly to unearth the ancient bottle, place it
shakily on a tray with two of the few remaining crys-
tal goblets the house boasted, then solemnly escort it
into the marquis's dazzling presence with a deference
worthy of a slave before a Roman emperor, they chatted desultorily of affairs at Oakley.

At last they were alone. Dolly had bowed herself
out, and the vicar had provided both himself and the
marquis with a goblet of the satisfying rich liquid.
"Now," said Mr. Dalrymple, "what business do you
have with me, my lord?"

Carrisbrooke had relaxed by now. The vicar's friendly manner encouraged him to speak his mind, the Madeira didn't hurt either, and the shafts of sunlight that filtered into the pleasant, shabby room spoke of intimacy and cheer. "I would like to ask you for your daughter's hand," he stated, his honest brown eyes boring into the vicar's face.

There was a short silence, during which a fly buzzed into the library and out again, little aware how its sound had echoed in the room. "Lord Carrisbrooke," Mr. Dalrymple answered in a plain, matter-of-fact tone, "does my daughter want to marry you?"

The marquis smiled in anticipation of mischief. Perhaps his favourite part of this plan was the thought of Sophia's surprise at his intentions, her probable outrage at being so tricked, and the way he would have to manoeuvre with all his military skill in order to bring her round to his way of thinking. "I believe so," he answered modestly. "I have every hope, though it will be a new idea to her."

The vicar nodded. "Then you haven't distinguished her in particular?"

Carrisbrooke bowed, willing himself not to burst out in laughter, which behaviour he judged would be most improper at this precise moment.

"Very proper, my lord," Mr. Dalrymple was continuing. "I must tell you, by the way, that my girl has been of age these three years and more. She doesn't need my permission to marry, though I know she'd want my blessing."

"And does she, do we, have it, sir?" queried the marquis in his most businesslike tone.

"What father in his right mind would turn off a marquis? You have my permission to try, my lord," responded the vicar, with an amused twinkle in his eye. "I happen to know something of your character, sir, and in every important way I think you the very sort of man to make my daughter happy. You've shown your bravery in the late war; Mr. Digweed tells me great things about your zeal in improving your estates; and if I don't miss my guess you're a very intelligent man. And aside from all these qualities, you've already done Sophia the very favour that was denied her by all her own relations." At this point the vicar indicated a stack of three small brown volumes which were placed conspicuously at one corner of his desk. "My daughter," said Mr. Dalrymple, "is a prize worth capturing. Don't you think so, Lord Carrisbrooke?"

Carrisbrooke mumbled that he was no novel reader.

The vicar stared. "But my daughter is a novel writer," he replied with a momentary furrowing of his brow. "Her work is the most important thing about her. Do you mean to say you haven't read this, man?"

The marquis studied the floor for a second. Then he looked up again at the clerical gentleman. "If you will but lend me that copy, sir, I'll read it tonight," he said stoutly.

"And you won't regret it," responded the vicar in approval. "I look forward to talking the book over with you. Do you stay a few days in Hertfordshire?"

The marquis took this statement to mean that, if he wanted Mr. Dalrymple's wholehearted consent, he would stay for a few days in Hertfordshire. He acknowledged such to be his plan and had soon gone away, the novel under one arm, to spend the rest of the day in seclusion at Oakley Park, bestirring himself only for a ride round the property and an excellent dinner served up in style by Amarantha's efficient staff.

The next day he was once again knocking at the door of the vicarage. This time he found Mr. Dalrymple sitting alone. After Dolly, without being told, had offered up yet another bottle of the precious Madeira on the altar of nobility, the vicar turned the conversation at once to his daughter. "Well?" he urged with a significant glance at the volumes clutched in Carrisbrooke's hand. "Do you regret lending your patronage to the child?"

Carrisbrooke said, with much feeling, "I can see that Sophia—Miss Dalrymple—has a rare talent, sir. We must do our best to see that she goes on with her work." He laid the volumes of *The River Garden* back on the vicar's desk. "She writes very simply," he mused, "but she sees very clearly. And the comic characters! I was in stitches over that pompous lawyer, who keeps begging Olivia to marry him."

The vicar nodded sagely. "She must be encouraged; I hoped you'd see that," he said. "I could hardly approve her marriage to a man who didn't think so. She has been writing ever since she was a little girl, you know, my lord, with her mama and me her only audience. That is, we were her only audience until she met Miss Helver—your niece's governess," elaborated Mr. Dalrymple. Suddenly his face reddened ever so slightly.

"I've met Miss Helver," said the marquis pleasantly. "I believe she's been helping out with the parish work in Sophia's absence?"

"Indeed yes. My daughter wouldn't have gone away if she didn't know she was leaving behind someone as dedicated as she is herself to seeing good done in this neighbourhood," replied the vicar. "Miss Helver has the makings of a saint, if you'll forgive the papist allusion, and she is besides a woman widely versed in literature and superior in understanding."

"I must talk with her about Sophia's writing," the marquis was inspired to say. The vicar's pinkness of visage bespoke some intrigue here, and it would behoove one who sought Dalrymple's good opinion to solicit that of a lady who stood so high with him.

"Glad to hear you say so, my dear sir," enthused the vicar, his face more colourful than ever. He picked up an enormous stack of papers from a small table set to one side of his massive old desk. "And here's something to help you in your discussion with Miss Helver—Sophia's first and second novels, copied out in her own hand. You'll be the third person to see these, my lord, after Miss Helver and me."

"Good God! All this?" cried the marquis with a smile, accepting the stack. "Murray will be pleased; he tells me we're expecting a great success with *The River Garden*. The kind of thing that sells small but steady, as he terms it, and leaves the readers wanting another of the same."

The vicar beamed, and after a little more time spent in discussing the merits of Sophia's work, the merits of the late Mr. Powell's Madeira, and the merits of Miss Helver, he waved the marquis out the door. Mr. Dalrymple's heart was light. His daughter would be well provided for after his death, and—what was more important—the man who had chosen her was head over heels in love with the girl. It didn't seem strange to the penniless clergyman that a marquis, rich in pedigree, landed estates and military honours, should wish to marry his Sophia. The wonder was that some lucky man hadn't snapped her up years ago.

The marquis went back to Oakley Park, ensconced himself in Amarantha's pleasant morning room, and delved into Sophia's manuscripts. He emerged only when dinner was announced. On an inspiration he asked the footman to summon Miss Helver to table.

"Have you been secreting yourself in your lonely chamber with a tray, Miss Helver, because you're too straitlaced to tolerate my rakish presence?" he asked with a smile, getting to his feet when the governess, in a hastily donned evening gown of serviceable dark puce, entered the dining room. "Have no fears for your reputation, madam, for hardly anyone knows I'm here."

Miss Helver flushed. "Well, my lord, it is a bit irregular for you to be staying here when I'm the only female in the house aside from the rest of the staff," she responded frankly. "Naturally I wouldn't presume to dine with you unasked. And don't think I'm worried for my good name. In a woman of my age, such thoughts are more pleasant than daunting. I'm sure I'll inspire nothing but envy in the old tabbies of the district when they learn I've been tête-à-tête with you."

He returned her pleasant nod, saying, "I'm glad you accepted my invitation, madam, however your good name might suffer. And no doubt you will know how to scotch any tattle-mongering. I wanted to talk to you about your friend, Miss Dalrymple."

Suddenly Miss Helver's eyes were gleaming in a manner Carrisbrooke had seen so many times in his sister and the dowagers of the Polite World that he couldn't mistake it. It was matchmaking. The marquis immediately warmed toward this good woman. "I've asked the vicar for permission to pay my addresses to the young lady," he informed her bluntly.

"Oh, sir!" cried Miss Helver in rapture, clasping her thin hands. "How romantic! I knew the dear girl would find the right man."

Carrisbrooke shook his head. "We mustn't be premature. I haven't yet applied to Miss Dalrymple."

"Oh, but Lord Carrisbrooke! Of course there can be no question," twittered Miss Helver.

"Do you think not?" queried Carrisbrooke with a studied casual air. He suddenly hoped that this maiden lady would make no references to his own superior station in life when elaborating on her flattering assurances of Sophia's acceptance.

"Of course, Sophia must be in love with you," Miss Helver was continuing with a faraway expression in her eyes. "I've often wondered why she would refuse so determinedly to consider her various suitors. Not that there have been many; the dear Dalrymples are quite penniless, and not many men can afford the luxury of an imprudent match. But *you* can, my lord." She smiled warmly at the marquis. "Why, the sweet child must have been nursing a secret attachment to you for years, little dreaming . . . Oh, how romantic," she cried out for the second time.

Carrisbrooke was pleased and not a little confused by these outpourings, and responded, "It's quite flattering to be the object of such an intelligent young woman's longtime affection, but to my knowledge, Miss Helver, Sophia had never seen me until I came into the district last summer."

"Oh, but she had," said Miss Helver with a twinkle. "She'd seen you years before, only once, but she was such a child at the time that it's no wonder her feelings of hero-worship got the better of her good sense. Oh, pardon me!'' she added, aghast at her last words.

The marquis grinned to convey his lack of offence, and pursued, ''I'm afraid I don't recall—''

''It was quite a small thing. She was a child in her teens, and she had climbed one of your trees. You saw her and chased her off the property.'' Miss Helver shook her head with a smile. ''The little incident occurred before she came back to school for her last term; and I still remember how amused she was as she recounted it. You took her for a village wench, it seems. I recall how I suspected at the time that my young friend was indulging in her first bout of calf love....''

Miss Helver's voice ran on, and Lord Carrisbrooke's mouth curved slowly upward into a smile. Sophia! That white, startled face surrounded by a tangle of dark hair, peering down through the branches of that plum tree. It had been Sophia! At the time he had imagined the apparition might be anyone from a dairymaid to a gypsy girl. How his future wife and he would laugh over the incident later; for he would casually mention the encounter, never giving away that Miss Helver's chattiness had recalled the meeting to his mind.

''I remember,'' he said now. Then, to turn the subject to the all-engrossing one of Sophia's future, he added with a touch of slyness, ''I hope that Miss Dalrymple will be persuaded to become my wife. I know she hates to leave her father alone.''

Miss Helver blushed painfully, and Carrisbrooke was satisfied on a certain point. ''Perhaps some arrangement could be made for the dear vicar's comfort,'' the governess faltered.

"I am sure we can do just that," Carrisbrooke responded with a wink that quite finished Miss Helver's composure and caused her to drop her fork.

Not a word more was said on this dangerous subject, and when Miss Helver had regained her calm and scholarly manner, abetted by an extra glass of burgundy, Carrisbrooke mentioned that he had been reading Sophia's earlier manuscripts. A spirited and laudatory discussion of these works followed, Carrisbrooke hanging on Miss Helver's words in a way that would have astounded any of his friends.

The next morning was Sunday, and the marquis strolled into the village, Miss Helver on his arm, to sit through divine service in the old square-towered church. This pastime was not in general a favourite of Carrisbrooke's, but he had indicated to the vicar he would be there, and he supposed that as the landlord of Oakley he did owe it to the villagers to distinguish their place of worship with his presence. The flattering attention bestowed upon him by these rustics was amusing, as was the ponderous sermon of the curate, Mr. Adolphus Penn. When church let out, the marquis deposited Miss Helver in the capable hands of the vicar and promised to join them both at the parsonage for a cold collation, as soon as he had paid his respects at the grave of his great-uncle. He was strolling round the side of the church to do this when he came upon the stocky, determined-looking figure of the curate, who was still clad in ecclesiastical vestments. Carrisbrooke realized that this near stranger was looking daggers at him, and immediately guessed the man to be a suitor of Sophia's.

"My lord, a word with you," declaimed Mr. Penn. His robes made him seem to swell as he planted himself firmly right in the marquis's path.

"At your pleasure, Mr. Penn," responded Carrisbrooke with a slight inclination of the head.

The curate stared resolutely at the marquis. He didn't like this handsome and haughty man, who was obviously steeped in the worst of worldly vices. Penn had never thought of Carrisbrooke as anything but a rake and libertine of the worst sort even before meeting him; and he did not stand in awe of the marquis's rank, as did some less spiritual beings, such as his hitherto respected mentor, Mr. Dalrymple. "I will not beat about the bush, Lord Carrisbrooke," he stated.

"Good," returned the marquis coolly.

"The vicar has told me something which I find almost unbelievable," continued Penn. "He says that you plan to ask for the hand of his daughter. Can this be true?"

"It is."

Something inside Mr. Penn seemed to snap; at least such was the marquis's observation as he saw the firm and hardened countenance of his rival slacken into something like dismay. That look was gone in a moment, though, and the cold mask was back in place. "Ah, I had feared that the good vicar had misunderstood your meaning, my lord," said Penn with a slight cough. "He is slightly hard of hearing. Well, it is my sad duty, then, to inform you that your suit would never prosper. Best leave it unsaid. Miss Dalrymple, you see, has pledged never to marry. She will not leave her father."

Carrisbrooke resisted the unkind impulse to tell the insolent curate that if Miss Dalrymple had refused

Penn for such a reason, her point was well taken. A lifetime of single blessedness in the company of such a well-informed and amusing man as the Reverend Mr. Dalrymple must be thought vastly preferable to even five minutes passed in the vicinity of this pompous stick. The marquis did not point these things out; he was too happy to be affected by this man, for whom he had only pity. The poor fellow had probably been nursing a hopeless passion for Sophia for years.

"If you say so, it must be a fact," said Carris-brooke kindly. "However, I am resolved to try my luck. Perhaps I can make the lady change her mind."

Mr. Penn's eyes narrowed, and his next words were ground out in a quiet, hate-tinged voice that contrasted oddly with the robe of his office. "She will never marry you." Then he turned on his heel and strode off down the graveyard path.

Carrisbrooke watched him out of sight and then continued on toward the tombstone of his great-uncle. What a quiz the curate was! Poor lovestruck fellow.

In the next instant Carrisbrooke had forgotten the disturbing Mr. Penn. His thoughts turned, as they often did, to Sophia. Would she prefer to honeymoon in Paris? Or would a quieter setting be more appropriate, a Mediterranean island where she might settle down to write? He smiled to himself. It would be difficult for the lady to find time from her wifely duties if her husband had any say in the matter, but he was somehow convinced that Sophia would manage her time very well. He envisioned her seated at a desk in some as yet unknown foreign part, striking out at him with her quill pen as he laid siege to her lovely white neck. Soon the quill would drop to the carpet, and so would Sophia and the marquis....

Carrisbrooke began to whistle. He was unaware that, from the shelter of the high hedge which bordered the graveyard, the unfriendly eyes of the curate were surveying him murderously.

CHAPTER FIFTEEN

"A VISITOR TO SEE YOU, ma'am," said Lord Carris-brooke's butler. "I have put the gentleman in the library. A Mr. Penn."

Sophia, who had been spending a quiet Sunday evening in the drawing room with her portable writing desk, started violently. Mr. Penn! What on earth could that tiresome man be doing here, and on Sunday, of all times? It must be some message from her papa.

"I'll go to him," she said with decision, rising and straightening her gown. As she made her way to the library she grew more and more apprehensive. That Adolphus Penn should appear suddenly in Grosvenor Square was so nearly incredible that she was beginning to fear some real mishap. Perhaps he had come to break news to her of an unpleasant kind? Her father...? Sophia had soon worked herself up into quite a state of nerves.

Nothing but this sort of thinking would have induced her to receive a gentleman alone at such an advanced hour of the evening. Sophia wished that Lady Amarantha and Echo hadn't gone out to spend Sunday with Amarantha's old aunt in Portman Square. But they had, and thus no one was by to lend moral support. However, it didn't take much to handle her father's curate. She had been doing it for five years, after all.

When Sophia opened the library door, the solid figure of Mr. Penn sprang toward her, and she involuntarily drew back. The gentleman seized her hand and planted a diffident kiss upon it while she surveyed him in amazement. His rumpled and dishevelled garb, his disarranged shock of hair and his dusty boots were eloquent in their announcement of a hurried trip. "Good heavens," she cried, "what can have happened, Mr. Penn? Don't keep me in suspense. Is my father well?"

"The good gentleman is in perfect health," replied the curate hastily. "Nothing like that brings me here."

"Then what is it?" asked Sophia in wonder. "To see you here, at such an hour and in such a state, sir, is so strange; and I know your feelings on the subject of Sunday travel."

Mr. Penn, avoiding Sophia's eyes, paced up and down the room for a minute. Sophia was inspired to take a seat by the fire and motion him to one opposite in an attempt to stop this irritating perambulation. But the curate declined to sit down, though he did come to a stop in front of her. His slightly equine features settled into a mask of sorrow, and he clasped his hands behind his back and sighed. "Ah, Miss Dalrymple, how to tell you?"

"How to tell me what?" demanded Sophia.

"I know you are the guest of the marquis of Carrisbrooke, and that you must have cause to think of him—at least in some minor way—with gratitude," elaborated the curate. "And to think that this man has betrayed your innocent trust in such an infamous fashion! He is a fiend.'' Mr. Penn resumed his pacing.

He had completed two circuits of the library before Sophia, failing to make sense of his words, queried, ''Are you saying that Lord Carrisbrooke has done something I wouldn't like?''

The curate came to a stop before her again and let out a dramatic, bitter laugh. ''If that were all,'' he exclaimed.

''What is it, then?'' cried Sophia. ''Sir, you're being deliberately obtuse.''

There was a short silence. The eyes of Mr. Penn, avoiding those of Miss Dalrymple, were engaged in examining the book-lined walls of the chamber. Sunday travel, and now an unadulterated, premeditated lie. But Miss Dalrymple's happiness must be his excuse. She must never fall into the hands of the libertine marquis, and she would not, even if a man of God had to jeopardize—a very little—his unblemished state of grace.

''You must know,'' intoned the curate, ''that the marquis has been staying down at Oakley Park.''

''Why, no, I didn't,'' answered Sophia, completely puzzled. Carrisbrooke had gone away to arrange for her country love nest, that she knew; and she believed him to be civil enough not to choose her home village as the scene of her future seduction. He must have stopped at Oakley for business reasons on the way back from his mysterious destination.

''Indeed he has,'' said Mr. Penn, ''and I swear the man must have gone mad. I knew him to be a rake, I suspected him to be wallowing in the very pits of degradation and shame, but I had believed that even such unfortunates, so lost to Christian behaviour, still had some remnants of decency...." He let his voice trail away, and he kept his gaze levelled at a point somewhere above Sophia's head.

"Good heavens, Mr. Penn, what has the man done?" snapped the lady.

"He has boasted, boasted quite indiscriminately, that he plans to make you his mistress!" There, it was out, for better or for worse, and Mr. Penn had no initial regrets about uttering the most outrageous lie, which his imagination had suggested to him.

"He hasn't!" gasped Sophia.

She was too overcome with shock even to be annoyed when Penn knelt beside her and took her hand. The poor man was only trying to comfort her in what he supposed must be her virginal indignation at such slander. Little did the innocent curate know that Carrisbrooke was only boasting of what was nearly a *fait accompli*. But "boasting"? That was so out of character for the marquis that Sophia was inclined to doubt the curate's terminology, though not his information. Perhaps, she considered after her initial shock wore off, Carrisbrooke had merely hinted in some obscure way about his proposed connection with Miss Dalrymple. It was still inexcusable, but something of the sort must have happened. Such a prime bit of gossip would naturally spread like wildfire through their quiet corner of Hertfordshire. Yes, that must be it.

"How did you hear of this, Mr. Penn?" she asked in a subdued voice, looking searchingly into the curate's slightly watery eyes.

Mr. Penn averted his glance for a moment, then looked straight at his companion. "From his own lips," he lied stoutly. Some old proverb about being hung for a sheep rather than a lamb drifted through his mind as he spoke the words.

"Good heavens," said Sophia weakly. Though she couldn't even begin to imagine the circumstances under which the marquis could have spoken of such a thing to Adolphus Penn, a man for whom he couldn't have the slightest affinity, she had no reason at all to doubt the word of her father's curate. Mr. Penn might be dull and humourless, but he was a man of God. He couldn't be a liar.

She sighed, and Mr. Penn patted her hand in sympathy. "I am ready, as always, to renew my earnest pleas for you to accept my hand and make me the happiest of men," he said, his familiar words barely breaking through into Sophia's busily occupied mind. "Say that you will be my helpmeet, dear Miss Dalrymple. You cannot refuse me forever."

Perfectly conscious that she could do just that with no untoward discomfort, Sophia gently withdrew her hand from his and, as usual, thanked her suitor for the flattering offer but was obliged to refuse. "You must understand, I could never leave my dear father," she said in elaboration.

"There, you see," exclaimed Mr. Penn, getting his solid form to a standing position with no little difficulty. "So I told him."

"Told whom, Mr. Penn? And what?" asked Sophia in consternation.

Mr. Penn's shrewdness and newfound skill in the art of mendacity stood him in good stead as he answered, with only a moment's hesitation as he searched his mind for a plausible response. "So I told your father when he suggested that someday you and I might marry. I repeated to him your feelings on the subject, which you have often discussed with me, and I begged him not to mention the matter to you." That last phrase ought to ensure that he wouldn't be found out in this latest, impromptu falsehood.

"Papa did that?" Sophia's look of blatant disbelief was perhaps not the most flattering reaction she might have given Mr. Penn, but she had no thought of that. Her world seemed to be turning upside down, and the only two men whom she considered worthy of her love were betraying her indiscriminately. That her father should suggest his curate as her possible mate was nearly as incredible as Carrisbrooke's going about boasting of his proposed liaison with her. But once again, why would Penn lie? "Good Lord," she whispered.

The curate, perhaps sensing he had gone far enough for one evening, immediately made his farewells. He didn't regret his hurried and wild-eyed journey to the metropolis, nor his indiscriminate bandying about of the only lies he had ever consciously told, for he believed that both circumstances had borne fruit of a most agreeable kind. Miss Dalrymple would be grateful that he had made a special trip to warn her about the marquis's infamy; and she would doubtless be prejudiced against Carrisbrooke's offer, thinking it a *carte blanche* or a hastily trumped-up substitute for one. And she would also be forced to consider the spurious fact that her father desired her to marry Adolphus Penn. Yes, he had done well to ride to London, the curate thought as, ever mindful of economy, he went to beg a night's lodging of a clerical friend in Soho.

Sophia sat and brooded for some time after Penn had taken his leave. How could Carrisbrooke have been so ungallant? Despite his promises to the contrary, he was apparently making free with her name throughout her home country. The blackguard! She dearly wished that she could back up her outrage with righteous thoughts of her own virtue, but this was not possible, and she grew even more angry as a result. She had to acknowledge that she *was* going to be his, er, paramour—she couldn't put a clean face on it. But she could still demand that Carrisbrooke rescind his horrid words in her own neighbourhood. No doubt a simple word to Mr. Penn would take care of this, for the curate would surely not spread abroad tales of his proposed wife's sullied reputation, and Sophia hoped that Carrisbrooke hadn't spoken to anyone but Penn. She intended to order the marquis to clear her name the very next time she saw him, which she hoped for many reasons would be soon.

Voices sounded in the hall, and leaving the library, Sophia met Lady Amarantha and Echo. The ladies were just removing their cloaks, and Sophia was very glad of the company in her present blackened mood.

"There you are, my dear," said Lady Amarantha airily, leading the way to the drawing room. "You know, I could swear I saw that tedious Mr. What's-his-name, the curate from the village, go posting down the street on a dreadful old spavined hack just as the coach set us down. I'm seeing things. It must have been the wine at dinner."

"Oh, Mr. Penn was here," said Sophia, who had already realized that trying to hide the visit would be useless. Every servant in the house knew about it.

"And what on earth did he want at this hour?" queried Amarantha. The ladies had entered the drawing room, and she now led the way to the fire.

"He must have come to see Sophia. He is in love with her," said Echo with a yawn, and she then sat down at the pianoforte and began idly drumming at the high C.

Sophia blushed.

"Indeed!" cried Amarantha with a lifting of perfectly arched eyebrows. She had lately come to value her daughter's ingenuous pronouncements. "And how long, my dear," turning to Sophia, "has this little romance been going on?"

"Five years." Sophia shrugged. "The man won't take no for an answer." She was very grateful to Echo, for she couldn't have thought of a better explanation for Mr. Penn's visit if she had ruminated for hours. And he *had* proposed.

Lady Amarantha sympathized. "How dreadful," she said. "Gracious me, Sophia, how many hidden strings does our vicar's daughter have on her bow? I vow it quite frightens me. First I find that you've written novels; then it comes out that you've been fending off an impatient swain of the stature of Mr. Penn." At this point both Sophia and Echo giggled. "What other mysteries are you busy keeping from us, I wonder?"

Sophia smiled enigmatically, wondering what Amarantha would say if she knew the kind of mystery that truly was being kept from her. The dear woman would faint, of course, at the thought that she was harbouring her brother's self-styled mistress. Or would she? Sophia asked herself with sudden insight, scrutinizing the worldly features of her hostess.

CHAPTER SIXTEEN

THE VERY NEXT MORNING Lord Carrisbrooke walked in on the ladies at their late breakfast table. "What a trio of sluggards," he cried in a cheerful voice, moving round the table to kiss his sister and niece and shake the hand of Miss Dalrymple. "I've been riding since dawn, and I'm hungry as a bear."

"Your appetite must be hereditary, dear," Amarantha remarked sardonically to Echo, who had been enjoying her usual large morning repast with stolid gusto.

Echo nodded in a vague manner. "Where have you been riding from, Uncle?"

Carrisbrooke shrugged. It seemed to be difficult for him to tear his eyes away from the blushing Miss Dalrymple to respond to his niece. "From here and there," he finally said. "Oh, by the way, I stopped in at Oakley Park on my travels and I can assure you that things are well in Hertfordshire."

So! That little bit of information seemed to corroborate, in part, the outrageous tale Mr. Penn had spouted last night. Sophia, under her blandest social smile, was suddenly seething. "Did you see anyone in particular?" she asked in the sweetest voice she could manage.

"Yes, indeed. Your father and Miss Helver, to name but two. I left them well," answered the marquis, taking a seat. He helped himself to the remaining kidneys from a dish Echo had already foraged in twice, then captured two stragglers she had overlooked in the kipper platter. "And what has been keeping you ladies busy?" he added.

"Oh, the usual," said Amarantha with a shrug. "You know, don't you, Charles, that Sophia leaves tomorrow? I can hardly believe the time has gone so quickly."

"Tomorrow! You don't mean it," cried Carrisbrooke. His dark eyes caressed Sophia with an intimacy which the young woman found distressingly public. "Then we must see that she soon comes back."

His womenfolk added their urgings to this, and Sophia shook her head and smiled. And she wondered, not for the first time, what excuse the marquis was planning to give her father for taking her off and seducing her. She was making things more difficult by leaving London. Unless... An awful thought suddenly struck her. Perhaps Lord Carrisbrooke meant to kidnap her en route to Hertfordshire, take her to the mysterious retreat which he had just arranged, and explain to everyone concerned that she was somewhere else. Yes, that must be it! She could think of no other way that he could possibly manage the project.

Sophia scanned the face of her future seducer with absorbed interest, trying to find some hint of his intentions in his features. He caught her eye and winked, and she looked down in consternation. Was tomorrow going to see the end of her long-guarded virginity? Her heart began to pound, and she knew that it wasn't altogether in dread of what might soon happen.

"It's lucky that this soirée of Murray's is tonight," Carrisbrooke told Amarantha, while another mischievous glance at Sophia escaped from the corner of his eye.

"What soirée, brother?" asked Amarantha. She was beginning to sift through the morning's stack of invitations.

"Oh, perhaps you don't know. Well, immediately before I came here I stopped off in Albemarle Street to make some inquiries of Murray, and he indicated that Miss Dalrymple—and you, sister, to be sure—would be more than welcome at a literary thing he's giving tonight for some of his authors. Don't you have the card?"

Lady Amarantha nodded. "We received it, but we weren't planning to attend. You know how Sophia is set against display, especially now that that horrid child there—" she waved her hand in the direction of the muffin basket, which Echo was excavating "—has bruited about the tale that Miss Dalrymple wrote *The River Garden*. Oh, but perhaps you hadn't heard?"

Carrisbrooke chuckled. "I have indeed but a few moments ago, from Murray," he said. "And I have to say I approve. Miss Dalrymple mustn't hide her light under a bushel. And now that the secret's out, Murray is naturally anxious to secure her presence tonight. She has the misfortune to have written the newest sensation."

"Then he's to be pitied we aren't going."

With a worried frown, the marquis sighed and said, "Had I known how strongly Miss Dalrymple and you felt on this subject, Amarantha, I wouldn't have told Murray I'd escort you both there tonight. Gave him my word, in fact."

Both ladies looked at him in exasperation. A short argument ensued, the outcome of which had perhaps been preordained. The altercation degenerated into a discussion of what the ladies would wear to the soirée, and Carrisbrooke left the table.

"I shall hope for a word with you later this morning, Miss Dalrymple," he said with a charming smile as he left the room.

Sophia, her irritation at his cavalier assumption of her acquiescence overcoming her curiosity at what he might have to say, resolved on the spot not to be at the gentleman's beck and call at any time that day. He needn't think she would rush to his side at his slightest whim!

Thus it was that by the time evening rolled round, the impatient marquis had not found one private moment in which to regale Miss Dalrymple with the interesting state of his heart. She had scurried from his grasp in the conservatory; she had turned on her heel and gone the other way on seeing him in the hall; and when he had burst into the drawing room once without warning, he had unmistakably heard an inner door shutting softly. It didn't take a genius to realize that Sophia was avoiding him for some reason. What the reason could be was a mystery. Cold feet, perhaps, at their arrangement? He had never before known her to stay away from him so determinedly. Was it possible that she no longer found him attractive?

ECHO, WHOSE INTEREST in works more literary than the latest dinner menu was negligible, was packed off to attend the opera with the same great-aunt she had visited on Sunday, and the older ladies and Carrisbrooke made ready for the jaunt to Murray's soirée.

As the marquis assisted Sophia into the coach he saw his chance for at least one private word, and murmured discreetly into her ear, "What can be the matter, my dear? We must find a moment alone soon, you know."

Sophia gave him a dangerous glance of disapprobation and said shortly, "I do have one request to make of you when next we have a private interview, my lord."

"A wonderful coincidence," exclaimed Carrisbrooke, "for I have one to make of you. I knew we had a lot in common."

Sophia gave a tight nod. She imagined he must have urgent information regarding their liaison. Perhaps a warning that her journey to Hertfordshire tomorrow would be interrupted in some way? She had to admit that such a prospect was thrilling as well as daunting, and that now she would have gladly listened to him in private. But she couldn't do anything but keep silent about the matter in front of Lady Amarantha, and in consequence the drive to Albemarle Street was spent in commonplace chitchat.

John Murray's comfortable house in Albemarle Street helped bear out the good opinion the world had of him. The salons were furnished in quiet, expensive taste, the staff was unobtrusively attentive, and it was evident that not only the sometimes motley group of novelists, poets and essayists were gathered there this evening, but a good sprinkling of the influential ton as well. Sophia, who had been in any number of great houses this season, was impressed. Carrisbrooke and Lady Amarantha were somewhat subdued; it was Carrisbrooke's first literary soirée, and though Amarantha had attended such gatherings before, she could not remember having seen quite so many lions in one place. When Murray strode across the drawing room to greet the three, a jovial smile bedecking his features, they were all looking at him with some wariness.

Ever mindful of etiquette, the publisher made his best bow in front of Lady Amarantha Burroughs, inquired after the health of her charming daughter and expressed his regret that the child was not present this evening. His acknowledgement of Carrisbrooke, the only marquis he had in the room, was similarly formal. Then he turned to Sophia.

"And this is our unknown lady! Our dark horse," the gentleman said with a conspiratorial twinkle in his eye. "Miss Dalrymple, I am charmed and enchanted to meet you at last. And I had no idea that my new authoress was a diamond of the first water! Come with me now, dear lady. A certain foreign gentleman has been reading *The River Garden* today, and he'll be very pleased to meet you. Do you speak French, by any chance?"

Sophia was murmuring an answer to the question—yes, she had taken French at school, but very little practical experience—as, in a bewildered way, she let Mr. Murray propel her across the room.

"That is a very determined man," said Carrisbrooke in an undertone.

"Yes, that's what makes him so successful," responded Amarantha with a sharp glance. "Well, I see some acquaintance over the way. Do you suppose Caro Lamb has been invited, Charles? Or that she'll dare to show her face if she has been? Well, have an amusing time, and if you can fetch a glass of champagne and bring it to me— Oh! Here is a tray."

And Lady Amarantha dove happily into the literary set, leaving her brother alone. She was well informed on the latest books, and it was enchanting to have this opportunity to further her knowledge. She had soon cornered no less a personage than Samuel Coleridge, and was questioning him on his *Kubla Khan*, which had lately appeared. Was it true he had written it seven years ago? Then Amarantha recognized Madame d'Arblay across the room; she had a slight acquaintance with this lady, and liked her. Carrisbrooke could see that his sister was having a wonderful time.

He could also see that Sophia, being steered from group to group by the thoughtful and admiring Mr. Murray, was in good hands, and he was content to watch her from afar for a while and play no more than an auditor's part in the proceedings. Not a literary man himself, he was content to observe those who were while he acclimated himself to a new situation. A little later, on noting that Amarantha and Sophia had fetched up in a little group by the fire, he strolled casually over to them, plucking a glass of champagne from the tray of a passing footman.

Madame d'Arblay was asking Miss Dalrymple where she had got the inspiration for her characters, especially that delightful lawyer—such a fine comic piece. Lord Carrisbrooke, who had recently listened to a sermon preached by the answer to that question, hid a smile.

"From my acquaintance, of course," returned Sophia, casting down her eyes so they would not meet those of the marquis. "I often find myself hitting upon one feature of someone I know in real life—a pair of eyebrows, a tendency to cough, that sort of thing—and then building a whole character out of my head to support that idiosyncracy. What do you do, *madame*?'' she added adroitly, thus turning the conversation to the views of the celebrated author of *Evelina* and *Cecilia*.

While Fanny d'Arblay expounded at some length upon this theme, Sophia noticed that Lord Carrisbrooke, rather than attending to the famous lady, was watching herself. He looked amused, which was perfectly natural. Though he was no novel reader, he couldn't have failed to hear the current gossip that the hero of *The River Garden* bore a resemblance to himself. It had been quite embarrassing for Sophia to have to speak of the origins for her characters in front of one such person, and everyone who had heard her probably knew this.

Suddenly the marquis drew her a little aside from the group and whispered, ''Was it my eyebrows? Or my cough?''

''Both, my lord,'' answered Sophia shortly and a bit mendaciously. She was certainly not about to tell him the truth: that he had so captivated her the first time she'd seen him, years ago, that he had been stealing into her fiction, in one form or another, ever since. To hide her confusion she directed her attention to the general conversation that had broken out among the little group. She did not have much success at this, as the marquis's nearness was disturbing her mightily.

One of the ladies was saying something about the absence of much pastoral description in *The River Garden*.

''Ah, very true, ma'am,'' put in Carrisbrooke. ''I noticed that myself, but with more pleasure than not. Miss Dalrymple's book is mainly concerned with the development of character. I am not well read on the picturesque, but I would say that the sort of book Miss Dalrymple writes is not ideal for that sort of digression."

"But she might try it next time," objected the lady. "I still remember the wonderful descriptions of the south of France in *Udolpho*. They might not have added to the story, but how captivating they were."

"And how totally hatched in the author's imagination. Was Mrs. Radcliffe ever in France?" asked someone else, and the dispute went on.

Sophia stared at Carrisbrooke in shock. The marquis, declining to spar about the question of the literary depiction of nature, was turning to an older gentleman who had been hovering at Sophia's elbow. This genial soul also seemed quite inclined to converse with the very attractive Miss Dalrymple, it being a treat to leer at the same person whose literary work one was discussing.

"And you, as her patron, must know this young woman's work very well," the gentleman said to Carrisbrooke.

"Indeed, I can lay claim to that coveted distinction," responded the marquis. "Now, the next book that will be appearing is quite in the same style, but it takes a different twist. The young heroine is orphaned and must go to live with some relations in a distant town. Much of the action turns on her total unfamiliarity with the place and the circle she finds herself in. A charming work. Perhaps the characters are drawn a bit more broadly than in *The River Garden*, but then it's an earlier piece, and besides as I understand it many readers prefer a less subtle sort of comedy. Now let me tell you about her very first novel, and you shall give me your opinion on which of these should appear next. Murray and I are in dispute about it...."

Sophia fairly gaped. To her certain knowledge, the precious fair-copies of her earlier manuscripts were still reposing in a drawer of the desk in her bedroom at home. How on earth had Carrisbrooke ever come by his knowledge of them? Had he actually tricked her father into giving them up? It even sounded as if he'd brought them back to London with him. And he had certainly read *The River Garden* from cover to cover, or so his knowledgeable chatter indicated.

Her dazed state lasted the rest of the evening. Over and over she listened to the marquis expound upon the subject of her work, with taste and flattering commendation. But for some vexing reason, he wouldn't meet her eye. By the time she, the marquis and Lady Amarantha had returned to Grosvenor Square, Sophia was wild to have a chance to be alone with Carrisbrooke and question him closely about his mysteriously complete knowledge of her novels. He had been evasive on the subject; in fact, he wouldn't say a word. Worse yet, he seemed to be avoiding Sophia's society all of a sudden. As she had been avoiding his all day, she couldn't feel ill-used, but she wondered what his reasons could be. In fact, she was mystified by everything the man had done tonight.

She didn't know that her face betrayed this mystification, nor that the marquis, observing how he had piqued her interest at the party, was determined to leave her in suspense for a while yet. He wished to heighten the air of mystery, and thus her fascination with him. It was a calculated risk, but he hoped that it would help ensure the success of the proposal he was planning shortly to make.

CHAPTER SEVENTEEN

AT AN EARLY HOUR the next morning Sophia was standing in the front hall of Carrisbrooke House, responding to the reluctant goodbyes of Lady Amarantha and Echo. Both Burroughs ladies were flattering in their insistence that if Sophia would not stay with them now to the end of the season, she must at the very least promise to come back for a final week in July. Sophia gave her word good-naturedly, reasoning that the end of July would surely have seen the end of her proposed intrigue with Lady Amarantha's brother. Not knowing the man's plans for her made things difficult. One could hardly say to the marquis's innocent female relations, "I can't swear that I'll be free. Lord Carrisbrooke might have arranged to seduce me at that time." So she left matters as vague as she could and trusted that absence would make the ladies forget the invitation.

"Now promise to write as your busy schedule permits, my dear," Sophia said warmly to Echo. "I'll be longing to hear about your *beaux*, especially Count Almirez."

"Yes," said Echo in sympathy. She was perfectly certain that everyone would be panting for news of such an interesting situation and felt sorry that Sophia couldn't stay to see the drama played out in per-

son. "And you must write to me, too. It will remind
me to write back."

"But you won't let your correspondence with this
child make you neglect your duty to me," broke in
Lady Amarantha, giving Sophia a hug. "I do hate to
see you go, my love. And it's so unfortunate that
Charles should be absent from home this morning. I
can't understand the man; he knew that you were
going." Amarantha was indeed vexed with her
brother. This neglect of Sophia augured poorly for the
quick betrothal she had planned for the two. Charles
had been very attentive to Sophia at the soirée last
night—Amarantha had been sure to notice that; in
fact he hadn't been able to keep his eyes off her! Thus
it was doubly mysterious that he should not choose to
bid her goodbye on the day she was leaving London.
Well, he must have had urgent business this morning;
that could be his only excuse. And if he was infat-
uated with Sophia he could ride out to see her in
Hertfordshire. It was a mere hour's trip.

Sophia also had her theories about why Carrisbrooke had absented himself this morning. The marquis was being maddeningly secretive about something; witness his avoidance of her last night after the
soirée. Rather than pulling her into the nearest empty
room for a surreptitious kiss, he had merely bowed
over her hand in the presence of his sister, then gone
out for a late-night gaming session at one of the clubs.
Was it possible that he had suddenly lost interest in
her? No, that couldn't be it. Sophia was rather cyni-
cal than not on the subject of men, and she couldn't
believe that any male would give up a certain seduction, even if not bowled over by desire for the woman
in question. Besides, he had given her that wretched

big diamond, which was now hidden in her reticule, as a symbol of his intentions.

No, there was only one explanation of his absence today that made sense: her suppositions of the previous evening must be true. He was planning to kidnap her en route to her home and take her off somewhere for the commencement of their amours. Despite her many unanswered questions about the man's behaviour, from his amazing knowledge of her writings to his apparent bragging about his conquest of her to the odious Mr. Penn, she felt her heart beat faster. She would have to be very watchful on the road.

Amarantha had ordered the Carrisbrooke travelling chariot for Miss Dalrymple's return to Oakley, though Sophia had politely insisted that she was well able to take the stage. Amarantha had laughed away this suggestion, but Sophia had at least been able to quash the idea that a maid should be sent along with her. It was such a short journey, and she so far past the schoolroom, that such solicitude was a needless waste of some poor creature's time. Amarantha, shaking her head as she gave in, had privately told the coachman to take every extra care, and cautioned Sophia not to step down at any posting houses, for if she were to travel as an unescorted female she must promise not to expose herself publicly as one. Sophia swore she would not do anything of the kind, ascended the coach in a flurry of kisses and farewells and began her journey.

As the carriage bowled along the London streets, slowly at first in the more congested areas, and then picking up speed as it reached the outskirts of Town, Sophia reflected that she had not really needed Lady

Amarantha's warning not to show herself in any public houses. At the rate the coach was travelling and the short distance involved, they would be unlikely to halt at all, except to pay the toll. Unless they were stopped by someone, such as the marquis of Carrisbrooke. He would conceal his identity, she mused, and sweep her up onto the back of his horse for a frenzied ride to their love nest, having first paid off the coachmen and postillions. Or might he not be more likely to offer his servants some fabricated excuse for taking Miss Dalrymple to another destination? The latter course would be more in character for the marquis; he would not care for the impracticality of an unnecessary masquerade. Sophia was in his own coach, after all, and he might direct it to go where he would.

Just as Sophia had begun to wonder, as a minor problem of her fantasy, whether the sober-looking coachman and the innocent-appearing postboys would really allow their rakish master to make off with a lady of gentle birth for purposes most foul—was their devotion to their lord medieval in its zeal, or were they rational modern creatures?—the coach came to a sudden, jolting halt and she was thrown into the seat opposite. She remained there while she righted herself and straightened her bonnet. Then she reconsidered whether she should open the door of the carriage. Rough voices could be heard grumbling at some length outside, but whoever was speaking was not in line with the coach window, and Sophia could see nothing but the rolling green expanse of field and the sunny morning sky. With an uneasy tremor she considered the many stories she had heard of travellers being set upon. Even this close to London, and in broad daylight, such things were not unheard of. But no, it *must* be the marquis who had stopped the carriage. She had thought he would, and it was really the only logical way for him to lay hands on her. She would get down at once and urge him not to befuddle his servants, as he was obviously doing if one were to judge from the protesting squawks that were audible just outside.

Her hand was on the door when it was flung open and a masked face peered in. "Your baubles if you please, madam, and your money," growled the mask in a husky voice which Sophia was certain was disguised. She was just as certain that neither the voice nor the steely blue eyes peering from the slits in the ornate, embroidered black party mask belonged to Carrisbrooke.

Sophia froze. She had been so sure that none other than the marquis would stop the coach, and now it seemed that she was going to be robbed by a common criminal. Through her fright she wondered why the masked man, who, apart from his mask, was dressed in the roughest of country clothing, should seem familiar to her in some indefinable way.

"Come along," the man growled, and Sophia returned to animation. With shaking hands she pulled her late mother's opal ring from her little finger and detached a gold locket from around her neck. She had no other jewels, and in her startled fear she quite forgot that the marquis's diamond ring was in her reticule. But when she opened her purse to remove her only money, the coins she had meant as vails for the postboys, she saw the black velvet box and gasped.

Another grunt from the mask recalled her to herself, and she pulled out her money and passed it into the leather bag the man held ready. He snorted as if in disgust at the paltriness of her possessions, but didn't seem likely to search her for more, or take her reticule. Her homemade travelling dress and plain, practical bonnet probably had something to do with that. He would think her a governess or a ladies' maid and let her go.

But to her surprise the highwayman next took a revolver from his belt, brandished it at her in a threatening manner and motioned her out of the coach with another guttural snarl.

Sophia trembled. Was she going to be shot, without warning and on account of such a trifling robbery? A flash of vexation that this masked character was not the marquis passed through her mind, and as she climbed down from the coach she couldn't help a resentful feeling that Carrisbrooke had definitely ill-used her this time by failing to abduct her in the manner of her totally fictitious expectations.

Another man, a squat, slouched-hatted fellow in rough attire was holding a gun on a grim line-up composed of the baffled and incredulous coachman and his boys, these last in varying stages of goggle-eyed fear, suppressed excitement and plain enjoyment. Sophia began to walk resignedly toward these prisoners to take her place beside them, but an arm shot out to stop her, and her masked friend slurred, "Oh, no, m'lady, you're comin' along o' me."

Sophia shuddered and glanced briefly at the horses, likely belonging to these highwaymen, that were tied up at the side of the road. Very showy cattle for desperate men, and expensively fitted out, she thought. They were doubtless stolen. Was she really expected to ride a-pillion to her doom behind this disgusting stranger?

"'Along o' me?' Come now, sir, you can do thieves' cant better than that," a crisp, familiar voice snapped out. Everyone jumped and turned in the direction of the sound.

Lord Carrisbrooke, his Town attire of bottle-green coat, fawn pantaloons and sparkling Hessians as impeccable as ever, and his neckcloth only slightly disarranged, was strolling around the side of the carriage.

Sophia gave a little shriek before she could stop herself, the coachman let a jubilant "M'lord!" escape him and the postboys grinned. How on earth, wondered Miss Dalrymple as she watched the marquis level a pearl-handled pistol at the midsection of the bandit, did Carrisbrooke come to be out here on the road? She didn't see a horse; there wasn't another vehicle nearby; there was nothing, in fact, but the Carrisbrooke travelling chaise standing in this lonely stretch of road.

The masked man, blustering incoherently, was pointing his own gun in the direction of the long-suffering coachman. Carrisbrooke cleared his throat and said in a plain, matter-of-fact tone, "On your way now, my fine gallows bird, and I won't reveal your identity to this lady. Nor will I mention this pretty scene to any of my acquaintance, and I am sure that I speak for my servants' discretion in this matter as well as my own."

At this point the coachman and the boys seemed silently to acquiesce in a body.

"Now drop your weapon and be off with you," the marquis repeated in the same conversational tone. "No questions asked. Was it a wager, perhaps? No matter, our lips are sealed."

The masked man uttered a short, pithy expletive in a clear voice, dropped his weapon at his feet as per Carrisbrooke's suggestion and turned on his heel. The other man, dropping his own revolver likewise, followed. They had soon mounted up and gone on their way, Carrisbrooke shaking his head in amusement.

The marquis then ordered the servants to ready the coach for departure, and taking Miss Dalrymple by the arm, led her a short distance away.

Sophia gazed up at him in consternation. "That was Lord Bell," she said excitedly. "I just recognized the voice, and was able to place those eyes. What on earth is this charade, my lord?"

"Oh, so you guessed," the marquis sighed. "Don't give him any hint that you did, my dear, should you meet him again, which is unlikely in the extreme. I believe I will shortly be suggesting to the gentleman that he might find the air of one of the German spas most bracing at this time of year."

"But what was he doing? Was it really a wager? Oh," she cried, as a sudden thought struck her, "he has my jewellery and the few coins I had by me."

"They will be returned to you in a few days. Did he get the diamond?" asked Carrisbrooke with a keen look.

Sophia was examining her kid half-boots. "No, it's still in my reticule. I didn't give it to him."

Carrisbrooke smiled. "Sentimental, my dear? Glad to see it. You're coming along." If she had been looking up, she might have seen that his glance was very tender.

But she had not seen his glance, and for once she was not to be put off by such digressions. "I simply thought that no highwayman would expect a plainly dressed female to have such a thing," she said with a conscious blush. "Now tell me, sir, do you know how this wager of Lord Bell's came about? Did he place a bet with someone that I wouldn't recognize him? I was never so shocked."

The marquis shrugged. "I've been having the man watched, thinking he might wish to devil you in some way," he admitted. "Unless I miss my guess badly, I'm afraid I just foiled an abduction attempt. Your worthy cousin doesn't seem to have accepted your refusal of his *carte blanche*. His minion, the fellow he was riding with, was easier to buy than most persons of that stamp, and I owe my knowledge of this escapade to his volubility and, of course, the excellent Mr. Mudgely's previous research into the baron's movements. No, there was no wager, my dear."

"And how did you appear out of nowhere, sir?" Sophia asked, continuing the interrogation. "I don't see a conveyance of any kind, but suddenly, there you were." She had no further questions to put to him on the subject of her noble cousin's perfidy. She was quite willing to believe that Lord Bell had tried to abduct her for the purpose of seducing her. Hadn't he been making her life miserable for weeks by his fumbling attempts to do the latter?

The marquis was smiling at her with conscious pride. "I was in the boot."

Sophia burst into slightly hysterical laughter. "So that's how you crushed your cravat," she was finally able to exclaim, wiping a tear from her eye.

Carrisbrooke put an arm around her shoulder. "Did I? Pity. I'd like to disarrange it further, but I'll restrain myself in the presence of my staff. Now, my love, hadn't you better continue on your trip home?

I'll ride on the box to the next village and hire a mount to take me back to London. I'd delight in a closed-carriage ride with you, of course, but every care must be taken of your reputation.'' And detaching his arm from her person, he offered it to her in a rather stiff manner that was belied by his twinkling eyes. He proceeded to escort Sophia back to the carriage.

"Very strange that you, of all people, should take such care of my reputation, Lord Carrisbrooke,'' Sophia was emboldened to murmur as he handed her in. She was astonished to find him so casual. It was vexing that he hadn't taken this opportunity alone with her—albeit witnessed from afar by servants—to tell her something about his proposed arrangements for her. She decided to be bold and mention the idea that had been in her mind all day. "Indeed, sir, I would have been shocked if my carriage had not been stopped in the road. But I expected it to be you, not my cousin.''

A hearty peal of laughter was Carrisbrooke's response to this statement, and he gave her such an affectionate look that she had to lower her eyes. "It would have been an idea at that,'' he admitted. "But in any event I'll see you soon. We have much to discuss.''

"We certainly do,'' agreed Sophia. Their future liaison, his shocking knowledge about her unpublished manuscripts and Mr. Penn's horrid tale of the marquis's gossip were uppermost on her list of topics. "But why can't we do it now?'' she asked a touch plaintively.

"Because I prefer to maintain my air of mystery for a while longer,'' answered Carrisbrooke with a broad wink. "However, it's only fair to tell you that I can scarcely contain my impatience. Well! A good journey, madam.'' And giving her gloved hand a cordial shake, he shut the carriage door on Sophia and climbed up to the box, there to take over the ribbons from his patient coachman for the brief stretch of road to the next settlement.

Inside the coach, Sophia was alternating between fascination and frustration. Had he been sure that such was Miss Dalrymple's state of mind, the marquis would no doubt have applauded his own success.

CHAPTER EIGHTEEN

THE REMAINDER of Sophia's journey into Hertford-shire was as uneventful as the encounter with the "highwaymen" had been exciting. Within a very short time she was being set down at the vicarage gate. Dolly flew out to meet her mistress, ecstasy at the presence of a crested vehicle shining in her pleasant face. Next to arrive in the small front garden was the vicar, blinking in the sun and fumbling for his spectacles as he beamed in the general direction of his daughter. "Sophia, my dear," he said in a voice of true wel-come, "how we have missed you!"

Sophia was instantly pleased beyond anything to be at home. She wouldn't long for London or wonder overmuch about the maddening secretive ways of a certain person. She was sure of that.

Half an hour later, when Sophia had changed to one of her favourite faded old round gowns and was pouring out tea for her father at the impromptu lun-cheon that she and Dolly had thrown together, she was even more certain that she would not miss the gran-deur of London—or some of its inhabitants—in the least. It was pure bliss to be at home, fussing around the kitchen and scheming to locate the least cracked pieces of china. Her critical eye noticed that the chairs could use a good polishing, and she felt her Town persona receding by the minute.

"Well," said Mr. Dalrymple, leaning back contentedly in his armchair, "when do you and Carrisbrooke tie the knot?"

Sophia choked on her tea. "Carrisbrooke and I?" she finally managed to gasp out. "The knot? Father, what do you mean?" In desperation she wondered if by any chance Mr. Penn had bleated out some hint of Carrisbrooke's evil designs to her father, who, in his innocence, had misconstrued the tale as an offer of marriage. How dreadfully embarrassing!

Mr. Dalrymple was instantly all blushing chagrin. "I was sure he must have asked you already, when he went posting back to Town to do just that," he stated miserably. "And now I've gone and spoilt his surprise. Well, you might as well know it all now, my dear. The marquis came to me to ask permission to pay his addresses."

Sophia, in her extreme confusion and surprise, could do no more than stare. "Are you certain, Papa?" she asked. "Might you not have mistaken his intention?"

The vicar smiled. "Not likely. I have only one daughter, and his words left no doubt as to his intentions." A note of regret came into his voice again as he continued, "How dreadful for you, my child! Your first knowledge of this should have come from his lordship, not your crack-brained old father. I can't help wondering why he hasn't popped the question, though. Perhaps he couldn't get you alone? He told me he hadn't been distinguishing you in particular, and it might not be easy to arrange a private interview in a houseful of women.''

Sophia shrugged. "He changed his mind, of course," she tried to say in a light voice. Her father's strange tale had overset her, and she was mystified at the same time. For the marquis of Carrisbrooke couldn't have meant to discuss a marriage between himself and a vicar's daughter. Her father must have misconstrued what had perhaps been a very responsible and probably technical discussion on Carrisbrooke's part regarding a settlement to be made her, or some such thing. She smiled at this idea. It was hard to imagine even such an audacious sort as the marquis discussing with Mr. Dalrymple the proposed ruin of the vicar's only daughter. Yet there must be some such dreadful misunderstanding here.

"Change his mind? Not he," said Mr. Dalrymple, with a warm smile at his daughter. "But do tell me, Sophia, will you accept him? I had no idea of your sentiments, naturally, and could but suggest that the man try his luck."

Looking down, Sophia murmured an indistinct monosyllable which had the desired effect. Her father saw her embarrassment and dropped the subject. Her mind was in considerable conflict, and she only wished she had the marquis in the room, so that she might chastise him for daring to open such a shocking subject as her ruin with her unworldly, saintly papa. She chose to ignore the very small corner of her mind that whispered how wonderful it would be if her father's tale were true and Carrisbrooke really had proposed marriage. Now *there* was a thought. He might have begun by talking of a *carte blanche*, she

reasoned, and been forced into shamming an honourable declaration by her papa's endearing refusal to
recognize evil.

In any case, she had the explanation of how the
marquis had come into possession of her manuscripts. When catechized on this subject, Mr. Dalrymple was quite proud of his contribution to the
course of true love, so that he had given the eager
suitor plenty of material whereby he might come to
know the object of his affection and her true worth as
an artist. The vicar was blithely unaware that he might
have acted dishonourably by rifling his daughter's
desk, and Sophia was too kindhearted to argue the
point with him until she had been at home for a while
longer.

Despite her extreme confusion, Sophia's joy at being
back in the country grew with each passing moment,
and she wondered how she could ever have stayed
away so long. The most trivial of household chores
had taken on a rosy glow when viewed from the lonely
grandeur of her silk-hung bedchamber in Grosvenor
Square, and she spent her first afternoon at home
beating the carpets with a vengeance. The reality of
domesticity, while somewhat different from the
dream, did help to vent Sophia's various frustrations,
and by the time Miss Helver walked over from the
Park to dine with the Dalrymples, the daughter of the
house was looking positively serene, an appearance
she owed to her bodily fatigue. She had put on one of
her new modish gowns in honour of her homecom-
ing, and her physical weariness in combination with
her becoming new dress caused Miss Helver to exclaim that her former pupil looked ethereally lovely.

"You have the look of a woman in love," twinkled the governess as the ladies sat in the parlour, the vicar still being at his wine. "Positively radiant."

"I'm merely tired. My eyes will hardly focus," Sophia said with a laugh, averting those eyes in a guilty manner.

"Well, my dear, whatever the reason, you look very nice. When Mr. Penn arrives to drink tea with us he'll no doubt be so besotted that he'll ask for your hand again on the spot," said Miss Helver playfully, "though perhaps he has some competition now?"

"Helvie, what on earth do you mean?" asked Sophia in considerable hauteur.

The governess's glance was penetrating. "Why, nothing," she replied. Then she turned the subject to the plays Sophia had seen in Town.

The vicar had indeed asked Mr. Penn to join the party in the evening, though he hadn't been able to work up enough Christian charity to invite the curate to dine; and shortly after Mr. Dalrymple had entered the parlour, his subordinate was announced. Sophia, whose last interview with the encroaching Mr. Penn had been so strange, had difficulty in mustering the proper smile of welcome. Penn's own expression betrayed a lover's happiness as he bent over Miss Dalrymple's hand.

"Ah, dear lady," he said smoothly, "how delightful to have you safely home from the metropolis. I knew you could not stay for long in that sink of vice and wickedness." He flashed her an intimate look, which showed that he had not forgotten the subject of their last conversation.

"It's good to see you again, Mr. Penn, for the last time we met *in London* it was such a short visit," Sophia responded.

Mr. Penn immediately reddened and glanced at the vicar, whose surprise was evident. The curate began to bluster something in the nature of an excuse.

"You went to Town, Penn? When did you find the time?" queried Mr. Dalrymple with interest. It didn't seem to him that Adolphus had been missing from his sight for a single day; and had he known of the curate's intentions it would have been so easy to suggest that the young man stay longer in London. The vicar shook his head in regret.

Misinterpreting this gesture, Mr. Penn managed to choke out a semicoherent tale of a sick relation in Town, adding that he hadn't been able to resist the opportunity to carry news of the vicar's continued good health to his daughter.

"Yes, yes," Mr. Dalrymple said, snorting. "Next time see that you inform me. You might easily have done one or two errands, and stayed on for a few days."

The stricken curate promised never again to stir a step without his mentor's knowledge and concurrence. Sophia, satisfied that she had flustered the odious Penn to the best of her ability, was able to settle herself behind the tea tray with some modicum of comfort.

When the curate took his leave later in the evening, his offer to escort Miss Helver back to the Park was cordially refused. The governess said that she had some private intelligence to impart to Miss Dalrymple before she left, and would thus wait for the footman who was coming to fetch her.

"Well, what is it, Helvie?" queried Sophia once Mr. Penn had made his exit. "If you really have some private thing to say, perhaps we can contrive to send Papa out of the room, but I suspect you only wanted to escape walking home with that horrid Mr. Penn. Oh, excuse me, Papa, what an uncharitable thing to say."

The vicar cleared his throat, and Miss Helver coughed.

"Well?" Sophia repeated when a short space of time had passed in this manner. She looked keenly at each of her nervous companions. "Good heavens, is something wrong?"

"No, no," cried Miss Helver, with a pleading glance at the vicar. "It is merely... Oh, my dear, your father ought to tell you."

Mr. Dalrymple cleared his throat again. "Sophia, the thing is that Miss Helver and I have it in our minds to marry. If you don't dislike it, of course."

"Oh!" cried Sophia. "What wonderful news." She sprang to her feet and hugged each blushing middle-aged lover in turn. "How could you think I wouldn't be thrilled to see the two people I care most about united? And Papa, in any case you must do as you like—you know that." She was beaming with pleasure as she went back to her seat.

Her father and Miss Helver had somehow rearranged their own positions, and were now side by side on the ancient settle. Sophia could tell that there was true affection in their manner toward each other, and she wondered why she had never before thought of a match in this direction. It really solved everything for both her father and Miss Helver. As for herself, she would, in a sense, be free.

With a shaky laugh, she said, "It would seem you've given the lie to my only excuse not to marry your curate, Papa. I always tell him I can't leave you. But when you and Helvie set up house together, that will be no reason at all." Belatedly she remembered that Mr. Penn had indicated, on his visit to London, that the vicar would welcome a union between his daughter and his curate. Could this marriage with Helvie have been Mr. Dalrymple's motive for trying to get Sophia settled in life, no matter how? She had meant to take her father to task for saying such a thing; she would someday, but not now.

The vicar, she noticed with surprise, was shaking his head. "Mr. Penn is a worthy young man in many ways, but he's not the one for my Sophia," he said with decision. "You two would never suit. He is not quick enough for you, my dear."

Sophia stared. "Then why did you tell him...? Why did you suggest that I marry him?" she exclaimed in wonder. Only a moment before she had decided not to allude tonight to Penn's statement, but her curiosity over her father's seeming change of tune had got the better of her. Had there been yet another misunderstanding? Her life seemed to be full of them today.

"Why did I do what? You must be dreaming, Sophia. How should I do such a thing?" asked her father, a blank expression on his cheerful face.

"Why... Mr. Penn told me... I was certain he said that you wanted us to marry," said Sophia, wrinkling her brow in an effort to remember that conversation in the library of Carrisbrooke House. "Could I have mistaken the matter?"

"You must have," stated the vicar. "No such hen-witted idea has ever found its way into my mind, let alone passed my lips. Obviously poor Mr. Penn has been chasing moonbeams. Or you misinterpreted something he said." The vicar shook his head, and his hand, to Sophia's delight, found Miss Helver's. "Poor young man. Crossed in love."

"I hope his noble rival won't be served so, Sophia," spoke up Miss Helver. "I'm persuaded your heart won't remain cold in *that* direction."

Sophia gaped. Did everyone in the world think that Carrisbrooke wished to marry her? It was reasonable, of course, for the vicar to have confided such a belief to his affianced bride. But it was distressing to find the false story spreading. Sophia's mind worked busily. Perhaps—it was a wild thought, but the only one which she could come up with—the marquis had decided to pretend to marry her in order to snatch her away from her father's eye for the seduction. They might get a false annulment, and her honour would be salvaged in a small way.

Miss Helver saw Sophia's confused and gloomy expression, silently diagnosed love troubles and accordingly changed the subject. "You haven't even asked us if we plan a long engagement, my dear girl."

Blinking, Sophia said, "And do you?"

"Why, no, we intend to post the banns next Sunday," replied her father. "Why waste time, since we're both decided?"

"And is this a new idea of yours, Papa? Was it my absence that brought you to a knowledge of Helvie's worth?"

"Why, to tell you the truth," said the vicar, his forehead reddening, "I've thought for some time that a match between Delilah and me would be the very thing. But Delilah was busy with little Echo Burroughs, and I meant every mark of respect to your lamented mama, and ... well, in short, now the time is right. Miss Burroughs is out of the schoolroom, and you are to be taken care of—"

"I hate to contradict you, Papa, but you must resign yourself to my continuance in your household," said Sophia with a sigh. "I'm not likely to marry." Nor to be set up for the long term as a Fashionable Impure, no matter what Carrisbrooke wishes, she added to herself.

The vicar and Miss Helver exchanged worried glances, but said nothing more on the topic. Instead, the talk turned to details of their own projected wedding, and a bridal tour to Cheltenham Spa was brought out for consideration. Dispute over this took up the rest of the evening, for the vicar was set on a proper honeymoon, while his daughter and Miss Helver were as adamant that the money could not be found.

"Unless," suggested Sophia in a moment of inspiration, "you allow me to make the trip my gift to you! It would be delightful for the two of you to have a honeymoon. I'm certain to have money from my book soon, and what better use for it?"

Her father and his betrothed were against such a course on principle, and so a new argument ensued.

By the time the evening was over the combatants had come to some sort of accord on the subject of the honeymoon, and all were in charity with one another at the thought that Mr. Dalrymple, his daughter and Miss Helver would divide the cost of the trip equally among themselves. The affianced couple soon walked off across the Park, accompanied at a discreet distance by the Burroughs footman, and Sophia sat alone in the parlour and thought over the day's events.

She was sincerely pleased that her father and her dearest friend were to find happiness with each other. But for some vexing reason, the exciting news made her feel lonelier than ever.

CHAPTER NINETEEN

THE MORNING POST brought Sophia the following letter from Lady Amarantha Burroughs:

My dearest creature,
The enclosed invitation will surprise you, I daresay. I know that you only left this morning, but already we are making plans to disturb your country solitude. You must know that this very afternoon Charles decided that the perfect way to enliven the season would be to make up an excursion up to Oakley Park for a sort of al fresco party. You may well ask why he wishes to visit that particular part of Hertfordshire at this particular time, but somehow I don't think you will. The other invitations are to go out tomorrow morning, to any number of our friends. Echo is adamant that not one of her collection of *beaux* be excluded, so you may look forward to a distressing number of bone-headed young men mooning about. As I pointed out to Echo, she knows very few young ladies, so I am having to use my imagination to give the numbers some semblance of evenness. Charles will be sending down his excellent Mr. Mudgely to organize the details of this entertainment, so do be kind to the

young man if you see him. This festivity is set for next week, as you will note, and Echo and I—and possibly Charles—will be staying over for the weekend. With all best wishes, etc.

Sophia was most diverted by this message, and she wondered mightily what the marquis could be planning now. Garden fêtes in Hertfordshire were hardly the rage in society; therefore he must have some ulterior motive. That he wished to have an excuse to approach her, she was certain; but what could he hope to accomplish in a crowd of cavorting young people which he could not do better by having a private interview with her at any time? Oakley was only an hour from London, after all, and he might ride there if he wished. His prospective paramour was already beginning to feel ill-used that he hadn't done so at the first opportunity.

That feeling was to grow in the ensuing days. Sophia went about her parish duties, cleaned the vicarage from attic to cellar and began to lend her dressmaking talents to a wedding gown for Miss Helver. She didn't find much time for writing, and what hours she did block out were spent in dreamy inactivity at her desk. She came upon Mr. Mudgely a time or two in the village and gave him suggestions about the party. And she studiously avoided Mr. Penn, who seemed to be lurking behind every tree. But through all this she was conscious of a smouldering resentment that Lord Carrisbrooke did not communicate with her. What could the man mean by being so mysterious? It was the outside of enough that he had given her father a spurious idea of his intentions; it was even more despicable that he should not clarify to Sophia herself his plans for her, which would doubtless be most complex and require elaborate plotting.

A nasty little voice in the back of Sophia's mind warned her that Carrisbrooke was absorbed in a new flirt and had simply forgotten her. Yet he was coming down to Oakley on purpose, and under cover of a large group of merrymakers. It must be to see her.

THE GREAT DAY DAWNED. The efficient Mr. Mudgely had spent the previous week in praying for good weather, and perhaps for this reason the sun shone as brightly as it ever had in an English June. When Sophia and her father strolled to the Park at the time inscribed on their invitation, the front sweep of the pink brick manor house was lively with arriving carriages and a milling throng of fashionables. Spotting Lady Amarantha on the front steps, Sophia led her father over to their hostess.

"My dears, I'm delighted to see you," cried the lady gaily, hugging Miss Dalrymple and extending a gloved hand to the vicar. "Such a charming idea of my brother's, don't you think? We are all to lunch under the trees over there; then it's to be a bucolic romp of shuttlecock and archery and such sports until we're hungry enough to dine indoors. Then an informal dance, followed by a moonlight drive back to London for those of our guests who don't choose to remain with us."

"How amusing it all sounds," Sophia said. "Where is Echo? And—" with a conscious lowering of her eyes "—I don't see your brother anywhere, either."

"Echo, Count Almirez and five or six young men have gone to explore the ornamental pond," answered Lady Amarantha. "There's safety in numbers, I always say. The child has never caused me a moment's real worry for that reason. And Charles is here. I just saw him a moment ago."

"Excellent. We'll wish to pay him our respects," said the vicar, noticing shrewdly that his daughter seemed quite unable to say more on the subject of Carrisbrooke. "Now, Sophia and Lady Amarantha, do excuse me. I see some members of my congregation over the way."

"He means he sees Miss Helver," Sophia whispered. "Did you hear about that little romance, my lady?"

Amarantha had not, and she showed just the proper amount of incredulity and joy at the prospect of the vicar's marriage. "And this will free you in a way, too, my dear," she added with a gleam in her eye. "Free you to marry, that is, with no fear that your father will be lonely without you."

"That will not be in the question," murmured Sophia.

Amarantha shook her elegantly coiffed head. "Such infernal modesty! Well, have it your own way, my love. Now do come and sit near me at luncheon. I need protection from all the young ladies and their mamas, who are indignant at my girl's success in drawing away all the young eligibles." She laughed, and arm in arm with Sophia, started the straggling procession to the al fresco tables.

The guests had soon organized themselves into informal clusters around the variety of cold meats, fruits

and syllabubs that Mr. Mudgely, in consultation with
Sophia and the Oakley housekeeper, had thought appropriate to the occasion. Echo and her court did full
justice to the viands, shovelling in everything at a great
rate, while the other guests—mainly jealous damsels
and their haughty mamas, as Lady Amarantha had
observed—made a great show of their dainty appetites.

As for Sophia, she had finally seen the marquis. He
had taken a place at the opposite end of the table from
her. She had been so nervous from the time she got up
that morning that by now her distress would not allow her to swallow a morsel. And it didn't help that
she felt various eyes upon her, especially the marquis's dancing dark ones, which, as might have been
expected, never left her face. But Lady Amarantha
was also looking at her keenly, and her father and Miss
Helver had her under surveillance—whenever they
could tear their gazes from each other. And naturally
Mr. Penn, who had to crane his neck to see her from
his place at a distant table, was staring with his normal besotted expression.

As soon as the meal was finished Sophia excused
herself to Lady Amarantha and declared her intention of taking a turn in the shrubbery to cool her hot
cheeks. "It is rather warm today," her ladyship
agreed. "If you want to find me later, dear, I plan to
judge the archery tournament. Have a nice walk."

Sophia sped across the lawn, her tamboured muslin skirts fluttering in the slight breeze. She had soon
ensconced herself in a certain rustic seat in the shade
of an ancient lilac bush. So quickly had she walked
that she was certain no one had followed her.

There had been no real reason for leaving the party, to be sure; simply a desperate urge to be free, at least momentarily, from everyone's amused, speculative eyes. Sophia's cheeks grew even redder as she remembered that the marquis had not even greeted her personally today; he had stared at her, true, but he always did that. Ought she to seek him out and demand answers to the million questions that were chasing one another around her mind, or should she continue to cower behind this bush? She considered the options carefully.

She had no sooner determined to look for Carrisbrooke than the ominous crunch of footsteps sounded on the garden walk. Sophia jumped up nervously. For some reason she expected that Mr. Penn had sought her out, and she didn't want to listen to yet another of his proposals. Scurrying round the lilac tree, she ran headlong into the marquis.

"Well, well! No need to scheme on how to get you into my arms." Lord Carrisbrooke chuckled, enfolding the shocked Miss Dalrymple in a short embrace. Then he set her away from him and smiled down at her. "I was looking for you. We must talk."

"That, my lord, is an understatement," retorted Sophia. Irritated, she looked at the ground. Her stupid heart had begun to beat so loudly all of a sudden that she was sure her companion must hear it.

"So happy that you agree with me," said the marquis smoothly, leading Sophia back to the bench she had just vacated and seating himself very close beside her. "I have already waited longer than I had expected to tell you what's in my heart."

Sophia regarded him with suspicion. "In your heart? Are you mocking me, then? You know that all we have to discuss are the arrangements for our liaison, though I admit I have one or two other questions to put to you."

The marquis's eyes were suddenly thoughtful. "Still on your high ropes with me for some reason? Do you care to tell me what the trouble is?" He took her hand in a manner that was supposed to inspire confidence, but in fact initiated a very violent reaction in the normally composed Miss Dalrymple.

For Sophia felt a superfluity of angry thoughts rushing about her mind, which she hadn't planned to put into words in a random and accusatory manner. But nothing seemed to matter at the moment but the distressing fact that this horrid man, whose touch made her weak, had been racing about the countryside engaged in one inexplicable plot after another, all designed, it seemed, to play havoc with her peace of mind.

"The trouble is," she said in a clipped, icy tone, "that you, sir, have been maddeningly secretive about your plans for our connection. You told me that you were going out of Town to get things ready. Yet when you came back you made no mention of any plans whatever, leading me to believe that you had changed your mind. Yet had you changed it, it would have been only courteous to tell me, so that I might cease to worry. And heaven only knows what strange tales you've been spreading about me in Hertfordshire, but the whole village, including my father, seems to have run mad. Lord knows what you said to him. And Mr. Penn, the curate, showed up in Town, before you were even back from your trip, babbling some story about how you were bragging of your intention to make me your mistress. He could only have got the story from you, it being perfectly true. And then—"

"One moment," Carrisbrooke interrupted, looking completely puzzled. "What's this about the curate?"

"Why, my father's curate came to Town and told me what you'd been saying to him about me," repeated Sophia. "And naturally I've been angry with you ever since. You promised, sir, not to ruin me in my own neighbourhood. You know I plan to spend my life here."

"Yes, as a poor but genteel spinster engaged in charitable work," said the marquis with an odd half smile. "I can't think what this curate person was about to tell you such lies."

"A man of God tell lies?" scoffed Sophia. "Why should he?"

"Because he is in love with you, perhaps? If you want the truth, Sophia, your father told the poor man that I planned to ask you to be my wife. Penn—is that his name?—then collared me and warned me that my suit would be useless, and when I announced my intention to try it anyway, he became quite angry. Perhaps he thought up the most outrageous, insulting thing that he could and hoped to give you a disgust of me—"

Suddenly Carrisbrooke stopped talking and let out a bark of laughter, covering his face with one hand for a moment and then peeking out through that hand to smile ruefully at Sophia. "I've done it now," he said.

"Slipped my proposal into a speech about the curate. Will you ever forgive me, my love?"

Sophia merely blinked. "But you don't want to marry me," she reminded him. "Don't worry, I've puzzled out what must have happened. You came to my father to declare your intention to set me up in style, or give me an annuity, or whatever it is men do with their mistresses. And poor Papa can believe nothing bad about anyone, least of all me. So he jumped to the conclusion you were a legitimate suitor, flung my manuscripts at you—for which I blame him very much, as he needed my permission—then told Mr. Penn what he honestly believed, and—"

The marquis stopped Sophia by placing his hand gently over her lips. "But I do want to marry you, my love," he said. "I always have."

Sophia made an incredulous sound midway between a sob and a giggle.

Carrisbrooke frowned. "Recalcitrant, are you? Do I take it you don't want to marry me?" His voice was serious enough, but a glint of amusement in his eyes betrayed his assurance and set Sophia's back up.

"I suppose you think you're irresistible," she said with a sniff.

"No," responded Carrisbrooke calmly, "not to everyone. Only to you."

"Oh!" shrieked Sophia. Really, the insufferable conceit of the man. How dared he have the unutterable gall to know how her knees weakened at the sight of him, how she felt full of life and spirit when he was with her, how his very touch sent fire coursing through her veins in a way she hadn't known existed outside the pages of lending-library novels! She was blushing deeply as she said, "That is perfectly untrue."

"It isn't. Now you might not relish being a marchioness, my dear, and I've thought of that. It is a lot of fuss. My mother was run off her feet at times, being the political hostess and chatelaine of the estates. But you'll be a different sort of marchioness. I'll give you all the time you need to pursue your writing. You must nourish your talent, my love. I know that now." The marquis paused. "And you will simply have to marry me, because you love me. It is even possible that you love me as much as I love you."

Sophia opened her mouth to make some cold retort, but closed it again without saying a word. She stared into the marquis's face, totally bereft of the desire to give him a setdown. He loved her! He had said so.

Noting this softening in the lady's manner, Carrisbrooke forthwith got down on his knees in the blessedly dry grass and clasped Sophia's hands in his. "My darling, this position might be more to your taste. Please be my wife."

By this time Sophia's sense of reason had reasserted itself, and she shook her head. "I ask you to make me your mistress, and you retaliate by demanding marriage? Something is wrong here, sir. Are you counting on my refusal? Is that it? Did Papa's belief in your honour embarrass you into doing this?"

The marquis got to his feet, pulled Sophia up without ceremony and kissed her, fiercely at first, then with more gentleness. "Will you leave your father out of this?" he finally murmured. "As I said before, I've always wanted marriage."

"Then why did you plan to make me your mistress?" demanded Sophia in the general direction of his neckcloth.

"Why, to tease you," responded Carrisbrooke.

Sophia's knowledge of the man she loved was sufficient to allow her to accept this reason without further elaboration.

"It was too good an opportunity to pass up," he went on, his mischievous eyes glittering. "You corner me in the woods and demand that I despoil you. Good Lord, it was probably on that very day that I decided you were the wife I needed. I'd never been so diverted in my life."

"But you can't have had such a plan. You kept telling me we were to be paramours, and mauling me about in a way that left no doubt as to your intentions—"

"Husbands have been known to pursue amorous relations with their wives," interrupted the marquis. "Not often, to be sure, but it happens."

"And then there was that diamond," continued Sophia a little desperately. She did want to believe that his intentions had always been honourable, but how could she? She still thought he must have only recently changed his mind, and this thought depressed her.

"The diamond!" exclaimed Carrisbrooke. "The very thing. Where is it, my love?"

"In the darkest corner of my clothespress, of course," said Sophia. "Why do you ask?"

"Did you never take it out of the box and try it on?" he pursued, ignoring her question.

"No," said Sophia. She had once or twice opened the velvet case to meditate in a troubled spirit on the shocking implications of the bright, sinful-looking jewel, but she had never dared put it on her finger.

"Then let's go fetch it now," urged Carrisbrooke. "My dear, had you but known, you've been carrying around with you absolute proof that my intentions were honourable when I left Town for my mysterious trip to the country."

"How can that be?"

"You'll see. Take me to see the diamond. We'll go by the orchard walk, and no one will miss us."

Certain that several people would indeed miss the host of the party and the vicar's daughter, and draw their own shocking conclusions, Sophia nevertheless agreed to make the short walk to the vicarage. Carrisbrooke grasped her hand and strode off in that direction, and she was soon busy trying to match her steps with his.

THE VICARAGE WAS completely deserted. Dolly had gone out to the feast that the excellent Mr. Mudgely had caused to be set up for the cottagers to coincide with the fête at the Park. As Sophia let herself and Carrisbrooke in at the back door, she was very aware of the solitude and its impropriety.

"Please wait in the parlour, my lord, and I'll get the diamond," she suggested nervously.

"No, I'll come with you," said Carrisbrooke, putting his arm around her waist. "In your bedroom, is it? Most daring of us, but we'll be married soon."

"Sir, I haven't agreed to that," sighed Sophia, trying to ignore her traitorous body's shocking response to the gentleman's nearness. Because she could think of no way out, she led the way upstairs to her modest chamber. Carrisbrooke unhanded her just inside the door and leaned against the shabby wallpaper, his gaze flitting from the narrow white bed to the black-paper silhouette of Sophia's mother that hung on one wall. And there, by the muslin-curtained window which looked out on the church, was a small deal table set out with writing materials, where Sophia's novels had doubtless been composed. Carrisbrooke turned his eyes to his lady, watching in amusement as she burrowed in her closet, came up from her search with a roll of stockings and finally unwrapped the velvet box. She held it out.

"Good," said Carrisbrooke with a smile. He took the box, opened it and plucked out the ring. The large diamond had a rather wide gold band. "How are your eyes, my love?" he asked.

"They are better than most."

"Read this inscription, then," said the marquis, holding out the ring.

Sophia took the diamond, held it close to her face and obligingly peered at the inside of the band. She let out a little cry.

" 'To my beloved bride. S from C,' " quoted Carrisbrooke in a low voice. "Well, my dear?"

At this point Sophia, to her extreme vexation, felt a tear roll out of her eye. "You might have mentioned I was agonizing over an engagement ring," she whispered with a slightly watery smile. "I've felt just like a Cyprian."

"With no reason at all, Sophia," said Carrisbrooke in mock severity. Taking the ring back, he slipped it onto her finger. Then he folded her into his arms for a very gentle, almost reverent kiss.

"And you're letting me out of our bargain?" queried Sophia with an innocent look, when he had finally released her.

"Bargain? Oh, that I should ravish you in exchange for my help in publishing your book. Well, naturally. I can't ravish my own fiancée."

There was a short silence. Then Sophia smiled. In effect, her expression might have qualified as a leer. "Is there some law that says you can't?" she asked.

Carrisbrooke's laugh rang out, and he reached out to crush Sophia in his arms. "My own, you're showing more abandon than I'd ever hoped to find in my marchioness," he said, kissing her. "And if I take advantage of this situation—mind you I'm not saying I will—do you know what must follow?"

"What?" asked Sophia in her most inviting manner.

"Our early marriage by special licence. You'd be forced to make an honest man of me without delay," stated Carrisbrooke. "In fact, that very consideration determines me to act on your charming suggestion and behave like a cad."

"Please be as much of a cad as you'd like," murmured the future Lady Carrisbrooke, and she relaxed, at last, in her lover's embrace.

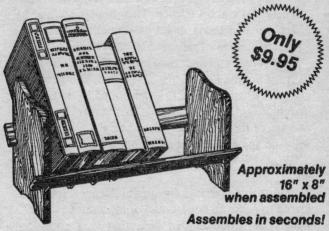

PAMELA BROWNING

...is fireworks on the green at the Fourth of July and prayers said around the Thanksgiving table. It is the dream of freedom realized in thousands of small towns across this great nation.

But mostly, the Heartland is its people. People who care about and help one another. People who cherish traditional values and give to their children the greatest gift, the gift of love.

American Romance presents HEARTLAND, an emotional trilogy about people whose memories, hopes and dreams are bound up in the acres they farm.

HEARTLAND...the story of America.

Don't miss these heartfelt stories: American Romance #237 SIMPLE GIFTS (March), #241 FLY AWAY (April), and #245 HARVEST HOME (May).

HRT-1

Penny Jordan

Stronger than Yearning

He was the man of her dreams!

The same dark hair, the same mocking eyes; it was as if the Regency rake of the portrait, the seducer of Jenna's dream, had come to life. Jenna, believing the last of the Deverils dead, was determined to buy the great old Yorkshire Hall—to claim it for her daughter, Lucy, and put to rest some of the painful memories of Lucy's birth. She had no way of knowing that a direct descendant of the black sheep Deveril even existed—or that James Allingham and his own powerful yearnings would disrupt her plan entirely.

Harlequin American Romance

Romances that go one step farther...
American Romance

Realistic stories involving people you can relate to and care about.

Compelling relationships between the mature men and women of today's world.

Romances that capture the core of genuine emotions between a man and a woman.

Join us each month for four new titles wherever paperback books are sold.
Enter the world of American Romance.

Amro-1
